Ghost Children

SUE TOWNSEND

Ghost Children

Methuen

Published by Methuen 1997

Copyright © Sue Townsend 1997

Sue Townsend has asserted her right under the Copyright, Designs and Patents
Act, 1988 to be identified as the author of this work.

First published in the United Kingdom in 1997 by Methuen,
Random House, 20 Vauxhall Bridge Road, London SW1V 2SA

Random House Australia (Pty) Limited
20 Alfred Street, Milsons Point, Sydney,
New South Wales 2061, Australia

Random House New Zealand Limited
18 Poland Road, Glenfield
Auckland 10, New Zealand

Random House South Africa (Pty) Limited
Endulini, 5A Jubilee Road, Parktown 2193, South Africa

Random House UK Limited Reg. No. 954009

A CIP catalogue record for this book
is available from the British Library

ISBN 0 413 68910 7

Phototypeset in Ehrhardt 10/12pt by Intype London Limited
Printed and bound in Great Britain by Mackays of Chatham PLC, Chatham, Kent

Papers used by Random House UK Ltd are natural, recyclable products made from
wood grown in sustainable forests. The manufacturing processes conform to the
environmental regulations of the country of origin.

To Geoffrey Strachan

November

Sleet filled the air and obscured the countryside.

He knew he was driving too fast. He was angry enough to kill or be killed. The road was wet and the metal signposts ahead warned him of hazardous corners and sharp bends, but he wouldn't slow down and neither would he turn his headlights on, even though dusk was falling.

Why ask *him* to sweep the snow off the fucking carpark? It wasn't his job was it? He was employed as a driver. Though why the fuck he was driving a van for a living, he didn't know. He had a degree in business studies. Three years of hard fucking graft. By rights he should have had at least one foot on the corporate ladder by now. He should be washing his hands with executive soap in a hotel somewhere abroad. He should be doing *business*, wearing the Paul Smith suit he was still paying for. *Paul Smith* and for six days a week it hangs in the poxy *wardrobe*. I'm twenty-seven, he thought. I should have my own fax number by now, I shouldn't be driving a van for a fucking nursing home, for three pounds seventy-five pence a poxy hour.

There was a red Audi ahead of him, crawling it was, crawling. It was a woman behind the wheel. He drew closer until he was tail-gating her, and saw that she was young, his age. *She* had a proper job, he could tell. Nobody would ask *her* to push a fucking brush around a carpark. She looked like the fucking tadpole carriers he ferried to the railway station in the nursing home mini-bus, three times a week. Sundays, Tuesdays and Fridays. No overtime for Sunday, and they wouldn't let him take the van or the mini-bus home with him. He had to stand at the fucking *bus stop* after work with the fucking *muppets* who worked in the kitchen. He'd worked out which car he'd have when he got a job commensurate with his qualifications. It was a BMW 325i, with veneer trim and leather upholstery. The doctors' carpark at the nursing home was full of BMWs. Killing tadpoles was fucking good business. He should have studied medicine.

She was mouthing something at him, her face was angry and frightened. To punish her he switched his headlights full on, then, although he couldn't see the road ahead through the sleeting sky, he accelerated and passed her. Looking back he saw that she had pulled into the side of the road against a bank of dirty snow. She was speaking into a mobile phone. He hoped she hadn't noticed the name of the nursing home on the side of the van. The bastards are not going to sack me, he thought. I'll resign. I'll take the van back tonight and I'll tell them I've been head-hunted by ICI. And there's no way I'm driving all the way across town to the incinerator and getting caught up in all that traffic, not now.

He turned on to the A6, and drove through villages where the old houses teetered on the very edge of the narrow road. He was calmer now that he had made a decision. As he drove he kept a look-out for a place where he could dump the bag which lay behind him on the floor of the van. About four miles out of the city he remembered that the heath lay ahead. He had taken a girl there once for a picnic. The sun was shining, and there were people about walking their dogs, but she had complained that the place made her flesh creep, so they had gone somewhere else.

The heath was in darkness now. He drove off the dual carriageway and parked alongside a hawthorn hedge. He switched the engine and van lights off, and sat for a while to allow his eyes to get accustomed to the blackness of the night. He got out and stood for a moment, looking and listening. It had stopped sleeting but the night was full of dripping and trickling sounds. A grey mist hung a foot from the ground. As a child he had been afraid of the dark and his childhood terror returned to him. He saw human shapes amongst the bushes and unmentionable horrors in the branches of the trees.

He went to the back of the van, squelching in the spongy ground. Wetness seeped over the tops of his shoes and he cried out in disgust. Ice-cold raindrops began to fall, soaking his hair and trickling down the back of his neck. He heard them drumming on the roof of the van. He fumbled with the lock on the back door. A harsh cry came from the black interior of the heath; a bird, or an animal. He waited, frozen, for the creature to cry out again, but the sound was not repeated. He opened the back door and groped in the dark for the bag. His hand touched the thick plastic and he recoiled from the wobbling sensation as the contents shifted slightly. He found the neck of the bag and lifted it out. He had planned to take the bag into the middle of the heath, but after only twenty yards of blind stumbling he heard a gurgle of water and threw the bag towards it. He heard it drop and settle.

When he turned around he was surrounded by a swaying mist of moisture. He could no longer see the trees or the van. He felt as though he was being sucked into the saturated ground. There was nothing he could grab on to to save himself. He turned around in a circle, stretching his hands out in front of him in a frantic attempt to feel something solid. A dark shape loomed ahead. He stumbled towards it and fell among the painful thorns of a hawthorn hedge.

When he eventually reached the safety of the van he saw that the thorns of the hedge had marked his face with bloody scratches. The rain on the roof sounded like an enemy trying to beat its way inside to drown him.

He started the engine and turned on the windscreen wipers, but they were useless against the relentless torrent. When he tried to drive away the wheels spun on the soaking ground beneath him and it seemed to take a lifetime before he was able to manoeuvre the van away from the vile place and towards the safety of the road.

One

The dog had always been a fool, look at it now, dragging a bin liner out of the ditch. The man shouted, 'Here! Here!', but the dog only stopped for a moment, then continued. As he got nearer he could hear a sound in the dog's throat. That sound, together with the look in the dog's eyes made him afraid, and he hesitated for a moment before reaching down and grabbing for its collar. The dog snapped at his right hand and in a fury of pain and anger he kicked the dog hard into its soft side. The dog yelped and dropped on to its belly.

Christopher Moore looked around at the dank scrubland. Nobody had seen him kick the dog. It was first light and dark grey clouds hung low enough to touch. Nobody else was walking their dog on the heath.

Anger made the blood drum in his ears. 'That's *it*, mate,' he said to the dog in the ditch, 'You've bloody *had* it, you're *off*. I'm having you put *down*.' The bull terrier was panting now, showing its powerful jaws and its long brown tongue.

He looked at the side of his right hand, where blood was seeping through a jagged wound. He hated to see his own blood, though I suppose it's proof that I'm alive, he thought. He turned his head away and moved from the edge of the ditch. He fumbled in his trouser pocket for the white cotton handkerchief and pressed it into the torn flesh. He could hear the traffic now on the dual carriageway beyond the dripping trees and bushes. The tyres on the wet road sounded like a pebbled shoreline. He wanted to leave the dog in the ditch, throw its leather lead into the scrubby vegetation and walk away. The dog crawled on its belly and attacked the dark green plastic again. The mouth of the bag came open. Something fell out and the dog pawed at it. 'Leave it! Leave it,' he roared and rooks flapped from a tree. Then he looked down into the ditch and saw a tiny naked child. It was a girl. Christopher climbed into the ditch and picked her up. She felt warm to him, but not warm enough to be alive. He placed her tenderly inside his coat.

Now he was close up he saw that the bag was more substantial than he had at first thought. The plastic was thick and was marked

INCINERATOR in yellow letters. There were other pink and bloody creatures in there. Christopher closed his eyes for a moment and then folded up the mouth of the bag. He pushed it back into the ditch. He couldn't take care of them all. He called the dog, which was lying on its belly, watching him, attached it to its lead and made his way towards the road.

He called her Catherine. He spoke to her, he said silly, jokey things as he trudged along on the pavement towards the small estate of private houses where he lived. His own voice sounded unfamiliar to him. He couldn't remember the last time he'd spoken to anyone. 'I live in Toytown,' he said. 'Wait 'til you see my house; it's like something out of a Noddy book.' Christopher had got an almost complete set of Noddy books upstairs in one of his spare bedrooms. They were flanked on the shelf by *Just William* and *Swallows and Amazons*.

The dog strained on its lead as they stood together on the pavement waiting to cross, and he jerked it back. But he wasn't angry with the dog now. If it hadn't been for the dog he would not have found Catherine. He would not have had a child to hold in his arms.

There were twenty-four houses on the two-year-old estate. They were known collectively as Curlew Close. No two houses were exactly the same, though each had a thatched porch and solar panels on the roof. Christopher hurried across the road and turned into the silent estate. He let himself in at the front door and went straight down the hall to the kitchen. He laid Catherine down on a pile of clean tea-towels on the work top, then, after washing the wound on his hand at the sink and applying a waterproof plaster, he fed the dog. When it was sleeping in front of the gas log fire in the living room, he took Catherine upstairs to the bathroom. He washed her in clean warm water in the wash basin. Her eyes were shut tight, but he imagined that they were blue. He compared her fingernails to his own and thought that he saw a similarity of shape. He patted her dry and wrapped her in a white hand towel.

He stood in front of the bathroom mirror with her and thought that he looked like the father of a new-born baby. Not dead, as he knew Catherine was, just sleeping, like babies do all the time. They're famous for it. It's what they do. He carried her downstairs and sat by the fire. His forefinger followed the delicate profile of Catherine's face. His finger looked grotesque to him, the skin was tough and forty-nine years old. Catherine's skin peeled away at the gentlest of his touch. She had been born too soon, before the thicker skin she needed to survive in the world had developed.

He sat there all day long until the room became dark. He ate nothing and drank nothing. When it was time to walk the dog again he laid Catherine on the sofa; he did not cover her face. He pulled the curtains, put on his coat, called the dog and left the house. He checked the front door twice before walking down the short path. Nobody else had a key to his front door. He never had a visitor. He walked in the opposite direction to the heath, towards what his neighbours liked to call 'the Village'.

Christopher had never called it 'the Village'. He knew what constituted a village and it wasn't a five-year-old pub, a dozen bungalows, and an executive housing estate grouped self-consciously around a primly landscaped lawn, with a Chinese take-away whose proprietor sent his children away to boarding school.

He passed the window of the Lotus take-away. On his way back he would tie the dog to the bollard on the pavement and go inside and order some food. His mouth watered, he felt light-headed, he had missed three meals.

When he got to the dark shape of the horse-chestnut tree which cornered the primary school football field, the dog strained forward and Christopher released it from its lead. The dog ran immediately to relieve itself, and he stood alone in the navy-blue darkness. He would give the little girl a decent burial in the morning: he might need to borrow a spade, he thought. This gave him a tremor of anxiety. He didn't fraternise with his neighbours, it was only as a result of a misdirected letter that he knew the name of the old man who lived next door.

Christopher's tiny back garden was covered in concrete slabs. He would have to lift one. Perhaps, if the ground underneath was soft he would be able to manage with the metal coal shovel he'd brought from his grandmother's house, three years ago. Tomorrow, after he had walked the dog, he would wrap Catherine in a single white sheet, cover her with earth, and replace the slab. He practised doing these things in his mind.

The dog rustled in the dry leaves at the base of the tree and Christopher smelt autumn. He took out the small flashlight he always carried in his pocket and directed it on to the ground. He looked for conkers and had soon gathered a pocketful. He had always contributed to the nature table at school but he had made his offerings secretly, when the teacher and the other children were out of the classroom.

He whistled the dog and it came to him, and stood obediently as it was put on the lead for the walk back along the road.

He would mark the grave. Perhaps place a terracotta pot on top of the slab. He wondered if November was too late to plant bulbs. He would look it up when he got home. His reference books were old friends. He tied the dog up outside and pushed open the door of the Lotus. Mr and Mrs Wong were reading the local newspaper, which was spread out on the counter covering the take-away menus. They looked up and smiled, and with some difficulty, because his mouth felt uncomfortably tight, Christopher smiled back. He was familiar with the menu and ordered immediately: spare ribs with chilli and salt – the dog enjoyed the bones – and prawn curry with plain boiled rice. His grandmother had warned him about eating foreign food. 'You'll ruin your taste buds,' she had said when, at the age of sixteen he had enthused about his first spaghetti bolognese. Now he thought she might have been right; English food seemed bland to him. He couldn't taste it.

After giving his order he sat down and watched the television, which was suspended high up in a corner of the room. The kitchen door opened and he saw Mrs Wong lifting a sizzling wok from the stove. On-screen a getaway car drove down an alley scattering empty-looking boxes. Christopher looked out of the window. The dog had wrapped its lead around the bollard. A teenage girl, dressed in a tiny skirt and a skimpy sweater which showed her midriff, was disentangling it. Christopher was shocked that her parents had allowed her to dress in such inadequate winter clothing. He thought about Catherine wrapped up warmly on the sofa. He had left the gas fire on for her. He knew she was dead: that it was illogical to worry about the temperature in the room where she lay.

Mr Wong was smiling again. Christopher took the plastic bag from him containing the small hot boxes and left the shop. The dog leapt up, excited by the smell of the food. 'Calm down! Calm down!' he ordered.

As he turned into the Close, he saw immediately that there was something wrong. He had left the downstairs lights on, but now his house was in darkness. The front door was open. He stood still for a moment, then sat down on a small boundary wall. He dropped the plastic bag on to the wet pavement. Prawn curry oozed out and the dog lapped at the food before Christopher kicked it away. After a moment he retrieved the bag, got up and walked slowly towards his house. Splinters of wood lay on the doorstep. He pushed the door wide open with his fingertips and let the dog off the lead. He reached inside the hallway and switched the light on. He saw that the phone was off the hook.

'We've been burgled,' he said to the dog. 'Catherine!' he said next. 'Catherine!' He felt his heart stop, and then start again. He ran into the living room. She was still there on the sofa, wrapped in the towel. He picked her up and walked around the house, noting what was missing: the television, the video, the computer, the microwave, his sound system, the cheap presentation watch given to him at the redundancy party to which he and thirty-nine other colleagues had been invited a year ago. He was glad the watch had gone. He muttered endearments to her as they walked around.

'There, chick, there, my little chicken, who's done this to us, eh? Who's been in our house?'

Her colour was bad now and the back of her head bore an indentation. There were stains on the towel in a colour he'd never seen before. He fetched a dry towel and wrapped her tight. He carried her upstairs. Other things had gone. The alarm clock, his electric razor, a travel bag. He couldn't bear the thought that a stranger had been in the same room as her. He didn't want to put her down; he needed to hold on to something.

'My chick,' he crooned. 'My pretty little chick.' He went into the bedrooms where his books were kept. None were missing. 'Philistines!' he said, contemptuously.

He laid her back in her place, in the corner of the sofa, and tried to plan what he should do next. He began to tremble uncontrollably. He found he could only think about food. He ate the tepid take-away food straight from the boxes, gulping down the rice and the remains of the curry and stripping the meat from the spare ribs with his teeth. He threw the bones on to the hearth rug for the dog. He wished he could pick up the phone and tell his grandma what had happened to him.

He had let all his insurance policies lapse. There was no question of claiming for any of the things stolen from him, and he didn't want the police in his house, not with Catherine here. After he'd finished eating, he went out to the shed in the back garden and found tools to mend the front door. The lock was broken but he found a bolt that would secure the door for the night; though he knew there was nothing of obvious monetary value left to steal. Nobody wanted his books, or the photograph of Angela that stood by his bed. These things were precious only to him. He went upstairs to check that the photograph was still there. It was in its usual place. He would try to find her tomorrow and ask her where his real baby daughter was. Angela was forty-six now. There would be grey in the black hair. The flesh would be loose around her neck. He wondered if she had any children, and if she still lived in the same city as him.

He didn't go to bed. He slept on the sofa and woke at six a.m., wet with sweat. The artificial logs in the fake Adam fireplace blazed with even flames. He drew aside a curtain, the window was covered in condensation. He wiped a small area with his shirt sleeve and looked out on to the empty Close, transformed now and made white and lovely by overnight frost. Christopher had a sudden desperate need to immerse himself in the cold air. He felt trapped with his memories in that loathsome house behind the double glazing.

He threw his coat on and clipped the lead to the dog's collar. He spoke to the baby but he didn't call her Catherine now. He knew she wasn't his baby. He wasn't mad. His baby had been born in June 1979. This was November and the year was 1996. He said, 'We're going out, chick, won't be long.'

Two

He half ran with the dog in the direction of the heath, their breath floated before them. He was aware of the smell of the dried sweat on his body. It drifted up to him as he walked through the sterile landscape. The bushes were hung with silver webs, like the doylies his grandmother had used for Sunday tea throughout his childhood. Christopher let the dog off the lead and broke off a twig from a hawthorn tree, bent it into an arch, and with great care lifted a frosted web from a bush. His grandfather had taught him how to do this. He would have liked to have demonstrated this skill to a child of his own.

When he saw the police Land-Rover parked by the ditch, he threw the twig on to the hard ground and called to the dog. But it was already running towards the Land-Rover and cocked its leg against the back wheel, yellow urine ran in a melting stream along the frozen earth. There were three policemen inside the Land-Rover. A side window slid open and a burning cigarette stub fell to the ground. He saw the policemen notice him and he raised his hand to them. Perhaps the gesture looked foolish to them because they began to laugh. He pretended to be absorbed by the dog as it ran out of sight. Then he heard the Land-Rover door open, and saw a policeman clambering out of the back.

'Morning,' said Christopher.

'Morning, sir,' said the policeman, who was putting on thick leather gloves. 'Are you a regular at this time of the morning?'

'I'm here most mornings,' said Christopher. 'With the dog.' He was suddenly aware of how he looked: unshaven, exhausted, his hair uncombed. The policeman was looking at the sticking plaster on Christopher's hand.

'At this time?'

'Bit later, usually.'

'And were you here yesterday morning, sir?'

'Yes, I was.'

'And your name, sir?'

'Christopher Moore.'

'Local, are you?'

'Down the road, Curlew Close. Number fifteen,' he added.

He kept his head turned away from the ditch, but when the dog barked and the policeman looked away he quickly glanced down. The bag had gone. The policeman pulled his right hand glove off with his teeth, and took out a Biro and a notebook and wrote down Christopher's name and address.

'You didn't notice a green plastic bag in the ditch here yesterday morning did you, Mr Moore?'

Christopher pretended to think. 'No,' he lied. He could feel the sweat trickling down his back and chest.

The policeman said, 'Can I ask where you work, Mr Moore?'

'For myself . . . I'm a bookseller.'

This was another lie, though it was something he had always wanted to do.

Christopher pushed his hands into the pockets of his anorak and wiped his palms on the lining. The dog came hurrying back along the frozen bed of the ditch. He shouted, 'C'm here!' and to his relief the dog obeyed him and scrambled up the slope of the ditch.

'Nice dog. Bull terrier?'

'Staffordshire.'

The policeman bent down and stroked the dog's smooth head. The dog arched its head back and rolled its eyes in pleasure. A woman known only to Christopher as 'red coat' came in sight with two Alsatians walking obediently by her side. The policeman left Christopher saying, 'So, if we need to talk to you?'

Christopher said, 'Yes, any time.'

He put the dog on the lead. It was afraid of the Alsatians. As Christopher passed the woman and the policeman, he heard the woman say in her hoarse voice. 'Yes, it was me who reported it. Yesterday morning, eight o'clock. It was horrible. I shouldn't have looked inside.'

He wanted to stay and hear more but he walked on. When he got home he crouched in front of the fire, he felt frozen through. He imagined that his bones were icicles and that his legs would shatter when he tried to get to his feet. It was snowing now. Christopher got up awkwardly and stood at the window and watched it settle. He hoped there would be enough for a snowman.

The fantasy came into his head that his daughter Catherine was alive and was watching the snow like him. She would be seventeen he thought. Too old for a snowman, but young enough to be excited by the thrill of deep snow. He shook the thought away.

He and Angela had never discussed exactly what had happened at the nursing home. He had not found the right words at the time, and she had volunteered nothing. Once, in the middle of the night he had woken and heard Angela crying quietly. 'What's wrong?' he'd said. 'Are you crying for the baby?'

'Baby,' she'd said. 'What baby? I've got toothache.'

He had got up to find some paracetamol for her.

He had a shelf full of books on child care and development bought from second-hand bookshops. He studied them in the evenings when Angela was out. She had never said to him, in so many words, 'The baby's dead,' only, 'After it was all over I asked them if it was a boy or a girl.' The abortion was very late, too late for the usual suction method to be used. Angela had gone into labour. It had taken her fourteen painful hours to expel the child from her womb. It would have been possible for the child to live; its lungs would have been formed, its heart could beat. Its brain would have been working, giving and receiving messages. Sometimes he dared to imagine that the child had been kept alive somehow, been taken away from the clinic and adopted. Perhaps he had seen her, had sat next to her on a bus? Miracles happened, he had read the headlines several times, 'My Miracle Baby'.

He shut the dog in the kitchen. Put his coat on and went outside to the small shed where he kept his tools. He selected a large chisel from the rack, where the tools hung in an orderly line. He found the metal coal shovel and went outside and cleared the snow away from a flagstone. He looked up to his next-door neighbour's bedroom window, the curtains were still closed. He would have to be quiet.

The flagstone lifted easily. The earth underneath was brown and friable. He used the chisel and the shovel to make a hole about a foot long and nine inches deep, then he went inside and picked up the baby. 'Hello, chick,' he said.

He wondered whose baby she was. It seemed wrong to lay her in the hole with nothing but a white sheet between her and the cold earth. So, he went in again, found a shoe box, and wrapped the little swaddled baby in two layers of green tissue paper, laid it inside and replaced the lid. As he lowered the box into the hole and raked the cold earth over it with his fingers, he kept his eye on his neighbour's bedroom window.

18

He had only five minutes before the alarm clock rang at eight a.m. and his neighbour opened the curtains. He strained to drop the heavy flagstone quietly into its place. Then he scuffed the snow around it. As he went back into the house he heard the neighbour's alarm ringing through the party wall. An hour later enough snow had fallen to obliterate the small grave completely.

He picked up several books, but found he couldn't read. With the television, radio and sound system gone, there was nothing in the house to watch or listen to, except the gas flames and the sounds they made. He was swallowing continuously. He kept thinking about the people he had lost in his life. He examined his hands. Since he had stopped working they had become smooth, his fingernails had grown again and he needed to cut them to stop them looking like a woman's.

When he was a young teenager he had worried about his sexuality. He had been afraid of the casual physicality of men. His grandfather had expected Christopher to accompany him to the Working Men's Club on Sundays, while his grandmother was at home cooking the dinner. They left the house together at 12.30 p.m. and returned at 2.30 p.m to the smell of roasting meat. In the intervening hours Christopher saw his grandfather coarsen and become boastful. Had even seen him threaten violence to a stranger who had inadvertently spilled his drink. He had had to force himself to laugh at the crudeness of the men's jokes and conversation. He would have preferred to stay at home in the company of the women who crowded into his grandmother's kitchen to talk about births and deaths and new scandals.

He went up to the bathroom intending to have a shave, then he remembered that his electric razor had been stolen. He took his clothes off and turned on the bath taps. He watched as the warm water crept slowly up the sides of the bath. A small mummified spider bobbed about on the surface of the water. Christopher lowered himself into the warm bath like a convalescing invalid. He lay still and watched the snowflakes as they passed in a diagonal pattern behind the small frosted window high up on the wall in front of him. Then he cupped his penis in his hands and fell asleep. He dreamed that everyone had died and he was the last survivor of an eternal winter.

Three

Christopher's mother, Audrey, was a pretty girl with a trusting nature that men exploited. Harry, Christopher's father, had been no exception. He told Audrey that she wouldn't get pregnant if she stood up immediately after sexual intercourse. Audrey, who had been shielded from what her mother called, 'owt like that', leapt to her feet three times during the first week of their courtship. Christopher was conceived a few minutes after his mother lost her virginity. Harry had no choice but to marry her. When Christopher was six weeks old, Audrey left him at the house of Harry's mother, May, saying she had an errand to run. She never came back. There were rumours that she'd been seen running along the canal bank in tears. Other people reported having seen her sitting in the front of a coal lorry, kissing the driver.

Christopher and his father had moved in with his grandparents, sharing the small bedroom above the kitchen, where on Monday mornings the steam from the copper boiler crept up through the floorboards, dampening the air and causing the wallpaper to peel away from the wall. Two years later Harry went to Canada to look for work. A few postcards of winter scenes came during the first year he was away, then there was nothing.

When Christopher was five he had asked his grandmother where his mother was. 'She's gone to see the world,' she said. He imagined the world to be where the film stars and the football heroes and the royal family lived. It became fixed in his head that the world and Pathé News were the same thing, and he believed that his mother must be inhabiting a Pathé News type of life. On his weekly visits to the cinema, he waited eagerly for the crowing cockerel to appear on the screen and the newsreels to begin. He scanned the faces in the crowds, even the foreign crowds, half-expecting to see his mother, but she was never there.

When Christopher went to junior school his class teacher was astonished at his extensive knowledge of Canada. His grandparents boasted to the neighbours about his precocity.

Once when he was a small boy, Christopher had dismantled his grandmother's cuckoo clock. She was outside scrubbing the front-door step, and washing the window-sill and the surrounding brickwork. But in that short time Christopher had sorted out the components of the clock. When she came back in she was astonished to see that the wheels and cogs and hammers, and the cuckoo itself, were all laid out across the chenille covering the kitchen table. He was equally curious about the solar system, the earth's core, the migration of birds, everything. The world seemed to him then to be a miraculous place. Ordered and planned on numerical systems that made sense. Everything could be explained. There were tables and charts to aid his thirst for knowledge in the ten volumes of Arthur Mee's encyclopedia which his grandfather had bought for him by paying six old pennies a week for three years. Christopher was numerate before he went to school. His grandmother unwittingly taught him to count by encouraging him to play with the hundreds of old buttons she kept in a Bluebird toffee tin. He spent hours sorting them by colour and size. He would form grids and columns and eventually he invented a hierarchical world where the brass greatcoat buttons ruled and the numerous white shirt buttons did all the work.

Christopher had no ambitions as a child, other than to go to work. The very word conjured up manhood and maturity. In the mornings he watched his granddad putting his work boots on. At night one of the last sounds he heard was the boots being taken off and dropped on to the wooden floor of his grandparents' bedroom.

He usually read until the early hours, only stopping when he could no longer see the print. Then he would close his book and switch off his bedside light and think about his mother and father. One of his favourite visions was of them dancing together, in a ballroom in Canada, to the tune of the 'Blue Danube', which he'd heard on the wireless.

Four

Angela Lowood stood at the bus stop and watched in impotent fury as her husband drove by without seeing her. The handles of the two plastic carrier bags she was holding cut into the palms of her hands. She turned to watch the car progress down the High Street. It was the evening rush hour but he would still be home within fifteen minutes. She almost moaned aloud with impatience, anticipating the long bus journey that lay ahead of her. But it was her own fault, she thought. She had urged him to borrow her car today, while his own was in the garage having the computer display on the dashboard looked at: it kept insisting that the driver's door was open when, to his rage, it obviously was not. It was her own fault that she had no gloves with her; her own fault that she had bought five pounds of Marks and Spencer's potatoes and two bottles of Chardonnay, the combined weight of which was threatening to snap the straining plastic handles.

She had watched the weather girl forecast snow on breakfast television, but had still left the house in the high-heeled bootees and Burberry raincoat she always wore to work in winter. 'Why didn't I put the quilted lining inside the raincoat? I'm inadequate and incompetent,' she said to herself; and warm tears of self-pity filled her eyes so that the bus appeared to her like a shimmering red mirage when it finally approached. When it was her turn to pay she couldn't find her purse. The driver stared straight ahead, blanking out her apologies. Women and their purses, it was an occupational hazard. The posh ones were the worst, he thought.

The other passengers queuing in the snow behind her shuffled impatiently. Angela moved aside to let them pass while she fumbled for her purse. Sweat drenched her hair and she felt a wave of heat suffuse her face. She searched frantically through her large black crocodile-skin handbag. It had to be there. She lowered the carrier bags on to the floor of the bus and tried to jam them securely between her feet, still searching. But when the bus started up, the contents fell out and slid along the floor. Angela gave a cry of distress. She looked into the faces of the other passengers and imagined what they saw: a clumsy, fat, menopausal woman with a red face.

'Sorry, sorry,' she said, as she bent to pick up the potatoes and the bottles of wine from between their snow-wet shoes and boots. An old woman picked up a packet of Marks and Spencer's frozen Yorkshire puddings. Angela saw her glancing disapprovingly at the price on the box before she handed it over.

When at last she had found her purse, paid the driver and struggled to a seat, she turned her head fixedly towards the window. Her blurred reflection stared back at her. A woman with a discontented mouth, tired eyes and long dark hair that she couldn't bring herself to have cut, although for many years there had been nobody to stroke it and tell her it was lovely.

Her husband had warned her before they married that he was an undemonstrative man. He had not allowed himself to smile for their wedding photographs, despite the entreaties of the hired photographer and the instructions of Angela's mother. His name was Gregory. He was seven years younger than her and one inch shorter and she had never called him 'Greg'.

When she got home he was in the hall, frowning at the thermostat. She dumped the bags on to the kitchen floor and kicked her bootees off. She didn't tell him that he'd passed her at the bus stop, or that as the bus had approached the top of their road she had finally admitted to herself that she no longer loved him. She put the groceries away and began to cook dinner. He went into the sitting room with the evening paper. As she put four lamb chops under the grill, she wondered how she would be able to live with him for the rest of her life.

When she went to tell him that dinner was on the table in the dining area, Gregory was sitting in his customary armchair, beneath the standard lamp under the yellow pool of light. He had removed one of the nest of spindle-legged tables and on it rested the local paper, turned to the obituary column. He pushed himself to his feet with a sigh and followed her into the kitchen. When she asked him why he was sighing, he said he didn't know. At five past seven he switched on 'The Archers'. There was drama in Ambridge when a pan of milk boiled over on the Aga. Angela looked at the place under the chimney where their own Aga used to be before Gregory took against its lumbering inefficiency. He had known somebody who was moving into a country cottage and had sold him the Aga and replaced it with a French cooker which had a deep-fat frier and rotisserie. He had bought the French cooker from somebody else he knew. His relationships with other people always seemed to consist of buying things from them, and selling things to them. He had once offered to buy Tampax, 'from a bloke in the trade', at a massive discount, but Angela had put her foot down and continued to buy her own from Boots. She was glad when her periods stopped, and she no longer had to endure his exaggerated intake of breath whenever he looked at the price sticker on the packet.

Another of Gregory's contacts had designed and built their new kitchen. The chairs and the oak table that he had done his homework on as a boy had been the only survivors. These were now incongruously surrounded by white and chrome surfaces. It's more like an operating theatre than a kitchen, thought Angela, looking around. They had been forced to knock a wall down to make space for the towering American refrigerator which dispensed ice and chilled water from a recess at the front.

She found that she couldn't look at Gregory's face: his moustache seemed ludicrous to her now, like a foreign object stuck on to his top lip. They had been married for seventeen years and there was no question of leaving him. She hadn't the energy to start a new life.

They were stacking the dishwasher together when the telephone rang. Gregory answered.

'Yes? Yes, she does. Who's speaking?' After a pause he put the phone down.

'Who was it?' she said.

'A bloke. Wanted to know if Angela Lowood, née Carr, lived here. I said, "Yes, she does." '

'Yes, I heard what *you* said.'

Now that she realised she didn't love him, she found his pedantry hard to bear. She dreaded the night ahead when she would have to lie in bed and watch and listen as he went through his bedtime routines: counting the change in his pocket, before placing it on the dressing table. Checking the alarm clock against the time pips on the bedroom radio, touching the radiator with the back of his hand, taking the bookmark out of his Ken Follett paperback.

'Who was it?' she repeated.

'*I* don't know, he put the phone down didn't he?' His tone was irritable, as hers had been.

They hardly every quarrelled, but the threat that they might hung over them for the rest of the evening. At twenty-five minutes to eleven, when Angela went out to put the milk bottles in the little crate on the doorstep, she saw a tall man in a long overcoat on the opposite side of the road. A barrel-chested dog stood in the snow next to him. The man and the dog were standing perfectly still in the shadow of a tree, looking at Angela's house. Angela instantly thought, 'Christopher'. But it couldn't be Christopher Moore, she decided: she hadn't seen him for seventeen years now.

As she moved from room to room turning off lamps, she could hear the shower going and smell the grooming products that Gregory had taken to using lately. His name was on file at the Clinique counter in Debenham's. He had recently started to send away for things like nostril-hair clippers and moustache trimmers from a catalogue called *Innovations*. He now went to a hairdresser called Henry's, for his monthly trim, instead of to Ron the barber's. He had even talked about having a light perm. Angela had been thinking for some time that Gregory's preoccupation with his appearance meant that he was planning to leave her for a woman of normal size. When she'd left Christopher Moore she'd weighed ten and a half stone. She was now nineteen stone and Gregory was half her size. They looked ludicrous together. It was for that reason that she wouldn't go to English seaside resorts, with their revolving racks of comic postcards. She preferred to holiday in America, where car seats, restaurant meals and Bermuda shorts were of more generous proportions.

It had been easy for Christopher to find her: one telephone call had given him her married name, and a second her present address and place of work. He was pleased to find that she had realised her ambition to live in a large detached house in a respectable area to the south of the city. She had put on weight, almost doubled in size, but when she had bent down to place the milk bottles in the crate and he had seen that black curtain of hair fall across her face, he had known for certain it was her. He had wanted to cross the road and speak to her, but he had not yet planned what he was going to say, so he stayed where he was. It was enough to be near her now.

He saw a light go on in an upstairs bedroom, then a small man with a large moustache approached the window and pulled the curtains together. Christopher experienced a moment of jealous rage. His fists clenched inside his overcoat pocket. He stood in the road, watching the window, until the dog pulled him away. The snow creaked beneath their feet as they embarked on the five-mile walk home together. The loveliness of the snow light affected Christopher. Joy overwhelmed him as he gazed up at the night sky and its brittle stars. He felt as though he could float up and touch them.

Angela delayed going to bed for as long as possible. She stayed downstairs, plumping cushions, wiping surfaces, folding tea-towels, and finally going into the conservatory and breaking the brown stalks and leaves from the over-wintering geraniums. Gregory called from the top of the stairs.

'Are you coming to bed or what?'

She went into the hallway reluctantly and looked up at him.

'What are you *doing* down there?' he said irritably.

'I'm not tired,' she said. 'I'll be up in a bit.'

'You *know* I can't sleep if you're not in bed,' he said. He turned away from her with slumped shoulders and went into the bedroom. She set the burglar alarm by the front door and went upstairs.

The coins lay on the dressing table in small towers. The bookmark had been placed on his bedside table. He looked up from his book, *Airship*, and said, 'About time.' She held her hair back and bent down by the bed and kissed him lightly on the forehead. She saw by the way his body relaxed that he was comforted by this ritual. He switched off his bedside lamp and arranged himself on the pillow with a series of little grunts. She wanted to weep in pity for him. As far as she knew, nobody loved him now.

She kept her back turned to him as she undressed, removing the voluminous clothes she had chosen from a catalogue endorsed by Dawn French, the fat comedienne. She kept her face turned away from the mirrored wardrobe doors. She had learnt to censor the reality of her naked appearance. She felt that she was hardly recognisable as a female human being any more.

They had been turned down by an adoption agency ten years before because she was too fat. Now she was three stones heavier and also too old. She struggled into her nightgown and went to the window and looked out. The man who looked like Christopher had gone, leaving only his footprints in the snow.

'Not far now.' The dog looked up at him as though pleased to hear this information. They were opposite the University, on the main road that led eventually to Curlew Close. A collection of teenagers burst out of the side door of a pub called the Swot and Firkin. Christopher remembered that the pub had once been called The King's Head. He pushed the door open and went inside; the loudness of the music overwhelmed him for a moment, but the young people inside seemed to be talking to each other without discernible strain. There was a young woman behind the bar wearing a t-shirt. When she turned her back to find the bottle of Guinness that he had requested, he saw that her back was emblazoned with the words, '*I'm Firkin tonight – Are you Firkin with me?*'

He bought a packet of crisps, ripped them open and tipped them on to the bare floorboards for the dog. The dog ate anything. Christopher stood at the bar and drank in silent celebration: he had found Angela. He could still see the slim girl he'd loved inside the fat woman on the doorstep. When her hair had fallen across her face he had suddenly wanted her again in spite of everything. Scraps of student conversations lapped around him. He looked at the back of the t-shirt worn by a thin blonde girl who was collecting a tower of glasses. '*Get your lips round my Firkin Ass*', he read. It wasn't right to make these girls wear these insulting words, he thought. He wouldn't have let his daughter be humiliated in such a way. A wave of misery enveloped Christopher. He pulled the dog to its feet and went out into the cold night.

Christopher woke early the next morning. He looked at the empty space where his clock radio used to be, then got out of bed and opened the thin blue curtains. The little light there was came from the snow. The sky was still dark. If he started to walk now he would be there, waiting for her when she arrived at Heavenly Travel – the agency where she worked. He dressed quickly, putting on the first things that came to hand in the wardrobe, unmindful of the weather conditions. A plaid shirt, a pair of thin corduroys, a short anorak, his old Adidas training shoes. He was too impatient to wash, or shave, or comb his hair. He threw some dog biscuits into the dog's bowl on the kitchen floor and muttered, 'Come on, come *on*,' as it crunched them between its powerful jaws. He ate nothing himself. As soon as the dog had swallowed the last biscuit, he attached its lead and pulled it towards the front door. His socks and shoes and the bottoms of his trousers were wet before he reached the dual carriageway. He was oblivious to any discomfort. A gritting lorry passed him and the driver raised a hand from the steering wheel in salute. You and me against the snow, it said. Christopher nodded in acknowledgment and turned on to the road that led towards the city centre. The occasional bus passed him, carrying a few early morning workers. But he wanted to walk, to make a proper journey of it, and anyway, he wasn't ready to rejoin the everyday world, not yet.

When he was two miles from the city the snow began to fall more heavily in large flakes that seemed to float rather than fall to the ground. The dog's back was coated in luminous white. There were occasional drifts where the snow came up to Christopher's knees, and the dog needed encouragement before it would plunge into the blinding whiteness. He passed people on the pavement who were warmly wrapped, and they glanced at him curiously. This odd man with his jacket open, no gloves, no scarf, nothing on his head, wearing training shoes and dragging a frozen-looking dog behind him.

When he got to Heavenly Travel it was half-past eight by the town hall clock. A sign on the door showed that the shop opened at nine a.m. He looked in the windows where the Winter Sun holidays were advertised. There was a poster showing happy, tanned holiday-makers on a beach in Barbados, the sand appeared to be white and the sea to be turquoise. He pulled the dog away and they went to stand in the doorway of a jeweller's opposite. To kill time he pretended to choose a ring for Angela from the wedding rings on display. He wondered why she had refused to marry him yet had married Lowood, the man with the moustache.

At ten minutes to nine he turned around to see that Angela was unlocking the front door of Heavenly Travel. He watched as she went inside and passed into a back room. The lights of the shop came on, but she didn't re-appear. He would wait for another fifteen minutes he thought, to give her time to settle in before he went inside the shop. Then he would ask her to tell him about the day she had their baby killed.

Five

Angela was at the computer trying to find a self-catering holiday in Greece for a pair of very shy gay men. When she next looked up, she was shocked to see that the man who had taken a seat at the counter beside them was Christopher Moore. She stared at him for a moment, then excused herself to the young men and went into the back room, where she leaned her head against a shelf full of City Break brochures. She would have to wait in there until he had gone. She didn't want him to see her like this: the size twenty-six uniform she wore. The light blue matching jacket and skirt had been especially made for her, at extra cost to the company. They didn't flatter her. The last time he'd seen her she had been a size twelve, and he had constantly told her that she was beautiful.

He looked terrible himself; unshaven and pinched with cold, as though he had reached the end of an arduous polar journey without the benefit of food and warm clothing. His hair was wet, and hung on his collar. His clothes were laughably inadequate for the weather conditions. His hands, which poked out of the sodden sleeves of his jacket, resembled defrosting joints of beef. There were three deep vertical furrows which ran down to the bridge of his nose, these were new to her, and she had a vision of taking a steam iron and pressing them out and making his face young again. It *was* him who had stood opposite her house last night and now he'd appeared at her place of work. What did he want?

After five minutes, a colleague, Claire, came into the back room and asked what was wrong. Angela lied and said she felt faint. She would go to the staff-room and lie down until she recovered. She asked Claire to find the shy young men a holiday and hauled herself up the steep stairs to the staff-room. She spread herself over three vinyl chairs and watched Christopher on the security camera. This was trained on the Bureau de Change half of the shop, but frequently swivelled around to show the customers waiting in the holiday section. Christopher was watching the door to the back room. He was waiting for her to come out. There was something about the stillness of his body that signalled to Angela that he would stay there, waiting for her, until the shop closed, if necessary. She knew that if she slipped out of the back door to avoid him that he would turn up the following day, and the day after that, until she was eventually forced to acknowledge his presence.

She watched another of her girls, Lisa, ask him to take his dog outside. She saw him shake his head. She guessed that Lisa was not afraid of the dog. It was Christopher she wanted outside. She knew that she would have to go downstairs and confront him, find out what he wanted.

She pulled herself up and combed her fingers through her hair. There mustn't be a scene. She would never get another job in the travel industry, not at her age and weight. Her long experience, her fluency in Spanish and German, and her expertise with international train and boat timetables meant nothing today. These skills were redundant now that holidays came tidily packaged, with one press of a computer key. As she walked back down the stairs, she recognised a tension within herself. A part of her was afraid of this disruption to her daily routine, another part of her was thrilled and excited by the prospect of a small personal drama. Before she reached the bottom of the stairs she knew that, whatever happened, she wouldn't tell Gregory that Christopher Moore had visited her at work.

She went straight to where he sat at the counter.

'Christopher?'

'Hello Angie.'

'Are you looking for a holiday?'

'A holiday?' He laughed at the absurdity of the thought of going on holiday. 'No, I want to ask you a question.'

'Go on then.'

'What happened to our baby?'

Six

They tried three cafés, none of which would allow the dog to come inside. Having agreed to meet Christopher for lunch, Angela grew more anxious with each rejection. She dreaded the conversation that lay ahead and they were walking east, further away from the city centre. She couldn't be late getting back from her lunch break. She wouldn't be able to hurry on the return journey. The pavements were icy underfoot. If she slipped and fell she knew from past experience that it would take at least two strong men to pull her to her feet.

As they walked they talked haltingly about the dog; what breed it was, its mild nature, how it had just turned up one day and forced itself into Christopher's life. 'It limped into the workshop and lay down on the floor. A young lad I had working for me bought it a tin of dog food. It came back every day after. I kept thinking someone would come and claim it. That's why I've never given it a name. I've never been a great dog lover but I wouldn't get rid of it now. It needs me.'

Like how I feel about Gregory, thought Angela.

By now they had left the city centre behind them and were being buffeted by the confluence of winds that blew around the twin towers of the city council offices. They walked alongside the inner ring road, protected from the speeding one-way traffic by a metal fence. In the distance, at the bottom of a gentle hill, stood the city's Ruritanian-looking prison. Security cameras were attached to the twenty-foot-high walls and Angela wondered if a prison warder was watching Christopher and herself on a screen as they walked down the hill. Opposite them now were the sprawling multi-levelled hospital buildings. The original Victorian red brick and slate infirmary was surrounded and dwarfed by the modern grey concrete blocks. Pale smoke blew at a right angle from the tall chimney of the hospital incinerator, like a long pastel-coloured flag.

Angela said, 'Can't you tie the dog up, outside somewhere?' She was tired of walking.

'Not in the town,' he said. 'Not if I can help it, this is the kind of dog that drug dealers like.' He slowed down. 'Good, it's still here,' he said.

They were standing outside a brick building that had been clad up to the first floor with black and white wooden panelling, in a grotesque parody of Tudor style. Above the black lintel of the Georgian-style door, somebody with a shaking hand had written in white paint, 'Veronica's Olde Worlde Tea Shoppe'.

'I used to come here with my grandma,' he said. 'After she'd been to the Outpatients over the road.' He peered in through the plate-glass window. 'It's changed a bit.'

A miserable looking woman, her greasy hair tied back with an office elastic band, stood behind the counter pouring tea from a battered aluminium teapot. She glanced up and Christopher caught her eye. He pointed to the dog and mimed that he wanted to bring it inside. The woman nodded and Christopher held the door open for Angela. Inside, there was a reek of rancid cooking fat.

Angela saw with dismay that the tubular chairs with the plastic seats looked dangerously fragile. She lowered herself to sit down with great circumspection, keeping her hands braced on the red Formica table in case the worst happened and the chair gave way beneath her weight. When she was securely seated, she looked around. It was a horrible place. Only the dark beams which crossed the low ceiling spoke of a former gentility. There were no tinkling teacups or saucers now. The tables were covered in packaging litter and spilt food. The red and white rubber floor tiles were coming loose. She moved an overflowing ashtray to an adjacent table. They looked up at the hand-written menu, which was scrawled on a board above the serving hatch.

Eventually Christopher said, 'What will you have?'

Angela's mouth watered for grease and carbohydrate and sugar, but she remained silent, unable to voice what she most desired.

Christopher said, 'I'm having the All Day Breakfast with chips and bread and butter.' This enabled her to say, 'Oh all right, I'll have the same.' As though her choice had been dictated by the wish to be companionable, rather than the need to satisfy her own greed. Eventually, after the ordering of food and mugs of tea, there were no more distractions. They looked each other in the face and Christopher asked Angela again.

'What happened to our baby?'

She looked at him blankly at first before saying, 'It died, Chris, you know that.'

Christopher said, 'I *don't* know that. I didn't see it, and you wouldn't talk about it.'

He looked out of the large window to the street outside. A young man with a shaven head was in a phone box. He was wearing a black leather jacket with a crudely painted devil's head and horns on the back. He appeared to be shouting into the phone. A small thin child in a pushchair waited outside, wearing a cotton romper suit and a short denim jacket.

'But you knew that it couldn't live, Chris. It was premature.' Angela pushed a track through the spilt sugar on the table with her forefinger. Christopher lowered his head to look at her face.

'Did *you* see the baby, Angela?'

'No, I didn't. I didn't *want* to see.'

He wanted to believe her, but he thought that she might be lying. He prompted, 'But you asked if the baby was a boy or a girl?'

'Did I?' she said, looking away from him.

'Yes, you did!' He'd raised his voice.

'Don't shout,' she said, looking around to see if anybody was listening to them. A couple of old women met her eyes before glancing away.

Christopher lowered his voice. 'The baby was a girl, you said.'

'For Christ's sake!' she said. 'Yes, they told me it was a girl.'

'Don't call her *it*,' he said angrily. 'Why didn't you want to see her?'

She didn't speak.

'Angie, have you ever thought, y'know, that the baby might have *lived*? Might be alive somewhere?'

Angela searched his face for signs of madness, but his expression was calm enough.

'No, I've never thought that,' she said. She knew that if she allowed herself to cry now she would never stop.

She took a tissue out of her handbag and wiped their table, accidentally pushing some of the spilt sugar on to the floor. The dog lapped it up immediately.

There was a long silence between them. Then Angela broke it, shouting, 'I didn't go in there to have a *live* baby, did I? I didn't *want* a baby, did I?' She no longer cared who heard her.

'But I *did* want a baby,' said Christopher. 'You had no right to take her away from me.'

Angela couldn't speak. A huge swell of tears was dammed up at the back of her eyes.

She got to her feet, knocking against the table in her hurry.

'Wait,' Christopher beseeched. 'Please don't go.'

She sat down again but turned away from him, saying, 'I don't want to talk about the baby any more.'

He tried to take her hand but she shook him away.

Christopher looked out of the window. The child outside, in the pushchair, was watching the shouting man in the phone box. Its thin face showed open misery. Its blanket must have fallen on to the pavement, thought Christopher. No responsible person would bring a baby out wearing such flimsy clothes. Not without a blanket tucked around it. Not with snow on the ground.

Angela studied Christopher's face while it was turned away from her towards the window. There was more grey than blond in his hair now, and the stubble on his cheeks was white. He looked like the ghost of the man he had once been. Only the colour of his eyes remained unchanged. They were still a peculiar shade of blue: 'like faded cornflowers', she'd told him once. She wondered when he had stopped caring about himself and why. He had been handsome once. Her friends and colleagues had been surprised when he had chosen her.

Christopher looked around at the other people in the café. It was a place where poor people came to eat cheap food, and smoke cigarettes, and rest for a while amongst their own kind. He understood this need. It was hard work being poor. It was almost a full-time profession. He'd been poor for a year now.

He couldn't bring himself to sell any of his books. He'd had some of them since he'd been a boy. He'd been given them by his grandmother and she had taught him how to handle them and keep them. It was a crime in her household to crack the spine of a book or to turn down the corner of a page. Later, when he began to buy his own, it was natural for him to select only those books that were in pristine condition. He was in his middle twenties before he realised that he had become a collector.

As if making normal conversation, he asked, 'Have you got any children?'

'No,' she said. 'Have you?'

'No,' he said. He wanted to say, 'Only the one *we* had,' but he bit it back.

34

The child in the pushchair was crying now and reaching its arms out towards the man in the phone box.

Angela was glad when the food came. She noted with satisfaction that the chips were piled high and falling off the plate, that the sausages were brown and fat, the yolk of the egg was runny, and that the strips of bacon had been fried and not grilled.

Crackle left the phone receiver hanging. He backed into Veronica's, dragging the pushchair behind him. The baby's head jerked as the wheels dropped over the sill of the door. It had stopped crying but was still trying to catch its breath. Crackle brought the pushchair alongside the empty table next to Christopher and Angela's. He used one hand to steer the pushchair, signifying by this slight detachment, that, though he was in charge of a baby, he still lived in the masculine world. Crackle went to the counter and Christopher saw that there were three sixes tattooed on the back of his head. He reached out and touched the baby's cold hand. He noticed that its fingernails were ragged and dirty.

The baby looked a hundred years old: its hair and skin looked desiccated. There were no plump folds around its wrists. It was a sharp-angled baby. When Crackle came back and sat down at the table the baby eyed him with a frozen watchfulness that reminded Christopher of his dog, after punishment. Crackle spread his fingers and twisted his rings so that the various pagan symbols: dragons, skulls, a naked woman, a devil with a three-pronged fork, a snake, were in the centre of each finger. It was something he did when he was bored, and there was nobody to talk to.

Angela ate quickly, she longed to be out of this depressing place. She didn't belong here with these people. She was afraid of Christopher and his questions, and she was repelled by the man in the leather jacket, and his odd-looking baby.

Christopher ate slowly, turning his head to look at the baby as he chewed. He couldn't decide if it was a boy or a girl. There were no clues. Its hair was straight and the colour of a page in an ancient book. The man took a Barclays cigarette out, then crumpled the empty packet and put it in the ashtray. He patted the pockets of his jacket, then raised himself and felt in the pockets of his jeans. He turned to Christopher.

'Godda light?'

'Sorry,' said Christopher. 'I don't smoke.'

Angela put down her knife and fork and felt inside her bag.

'I've got one,' she said through a mouthful of food. She found her lighter and flicked the flame and held it out towards him. She could see that the pores of his skin were clogged with dirt. As he leaned towards her, a smell like a sour dishcloth came from him. He inhaled deeply and nodded his thanks. The baby's hands curled open and then closed again, like a plant on the sea bed.

Christopher said, 'You've still got it.'

Angela handed him the heavy gold lighter.

'I don't lose things,' she said.

Christopher turned the lighter upside down and read the inscription on the base. *'For ever'* he read to himself. He handed it back to her.

'Still smoking?' he asked.

'Only now and again,' she said. She pushed her empty plate to one side. She wanted a cigarette now. She looked around for a machine, but didn't see one.

He'd given the lighter to her in 1978 in a hotel room in Paris after they'd spent a frustrating day trying out their night-school French. Reading it, speaking it, and understanding the measured tones of Mrs Humphreys, their night-school teacher, had been no problem. But they had despaired of understanding the real, rapid French, as spoken by busy waiters and shop assistants. Angela lay on the narrow bed in their seventh-floor attic room looking despondently through the guidebook that Christopher had bought at Waterloo station. He had planned to give her the lighter on her birthday the following morning, as they sat at the pavement café outside their hotel. But, on impulse, he went to his overnight bag, unzipped a compartment, felt inside and drew out a maroon leather box with 'Colibri' in gold letters written on the front.

When he gave it to her she sat up straight and opened the hinged box and cried out in delight when she saw the quality of the gold and felt its weight in her hand. She immediately lit a cigarette and smiled happily through the smoke, relieved for him that the lighter had worked first time, delivering an even blue flame after the slightest depression of the sleek side. It said 'quality' to her and she was pleased by this evidence that Christopher was perhaps, at last, letting go of his working-class background and tastes.

But, the next morning, when he asked her to marry him she refused. She loved him, but she couldn't marry a man who pronounced 'baths' to rhyme with 'maths', and was part-owner of a two-man electrical repair business on an industrial estate plagued by vandalism. She had been brought up to marry a man who wore a suit to work, who sat behind a desk, not a workbench. She couldn't say any of this to Christopher. She told him instead that marriage was an old-fashioned institution and that she was a modern woman. He had believed her.

Their baby had been conceived in the narrow bed to the sound of trains arriving at, and departing from the Gare du Nord. Uncharacteristically she had left her dutch cap in the bathroom cabinet at home and Christopher's French had not been understood when he went into a chemist's shop to buy a condom, and, desperate though he was, he couldn't bring himself to mime what it was he wanted.

'*Imbécile*,' she had laughed, pronouncing it the French way. 'You should have just said, "*Durex*".' Before they made love they agreed to use *coitus interruptus* as a method of birth control. Angela was adamant that she didn't want a baby. But, when the time came for Christopher to withdraw from Angela, he had been unable to do so. She was furious with him and pushed him off her, and lay at the very edge of the bed for the rest of the night.

Christopher speared a rasher of bacon on his fork and held it out to the dog under the table. The baby and Crackle watched as the dog ate.

Crackle said, 'Staffie 'int it? My mate's got one. It killed one of them little dogs last week. One of them foreign dogs what have got no hair.'

Angela started to hunt through her bag for her purse. She would pay the bill and go back to work. She would wait until she was behind the locked bathroom door at home before she allowed herself to cry.

The greasy woman came from behind the counter with Crackle's food. She placed it wordlessly on the table, watched by the baby.

'It torn its throat out,' said Crackle, jiggling his crossed-over leg in excitement. 'Weren't the staffie's fault, were it? Can't blame the dog. Bred to it ain't they, staffies?'

Christopher bent down and stroked the dog's soft ears.

Crackle took a long pale chip from his plate and held it out to the baby, who looked at it, but didn't move.

'Tek it, go on. Tek it,' said Crackle, irritably.

'His hands are too cold, I think,' said Christopher, guessing at the baby's sex.

'It's a girl,' corrected Crackle. He placed the chip on the baby's lap. 'Tek it or leave it,' he said.

'What's *your* name?' Christopher asked the still and silent child.

'Storme,' obliged Crackle. 'Storm, like bad weather, only it's got a "e" on the end.'

Angela rolled her eyes. 'Storme,' she thought. She had never seen a child with a more inappropriate name.

Crackle said, 'We called her after the one on the telly.' He broke off to stuff a forkful of chips into his mouth. Angela had seen the programme. Gregory watched it every Saturday without fail. Professionally athletic men and women in well-cut leotards competed with less beautiful members of the public, over a series of spectacular, but silly games, watched by an hysterical studio audience. Storme was a tall, muscled blonde. Gregory's favourite. Angela usually did the ironing in the kitchen while it was on.

'I must go back now,' she said to Christopher.

'I'll walk with you,' he said.

'No, stay and finish your tea,' she said, pushing herself to her feet. She wanted to be by herself. She calculated the gaps between the chairs and tables. She would not be able to get to the door without asking people to move. She put a £10 note on the table. Christopher looked as if he might be short of money.

'Bye then, Chris.'

He told the dog, 'Stay', and got up and went before her, making a tactful path for her bulk. He opened the door for her, and they stood together on the pavement in the shockingly cold air.

Christopher said, 'I'll come to see you again.'

Angela said, 'No, don't', and shook her head. Her hair fell in front of her face and he reached out and held the heaviness of it for a moment. He loved her again. She turned the collar of her coat up, and tucked her hair inside. 'I'm late now,' she said, and turned and walked off in the direction of the agency, treading cautiously on the icy pavement.

Seven

Tamara put the phone down and wiped her eyes on a piece of crumpled toilet paper. Honest. That Crackle! she thought. How was she supposed to get down town by half-past one? She didn't have the bus fare and she'd rung her dad for a lift, but he weren't at home and now she was trapped in the flat. She couldn't go out. That guy sitting in the car outside had come to serve a warrant on her. He would get her if she left now. He would trick her by using long words. She couldn't use long words herself. They wouldn't stay in her head. If she tried to use them they got jumbled up on her tongue and came out wrong. She only ever used the little words she'd used as a child. She would have to wait until the man in the car had gone. Crackle had gone mad on the phone. She hated it when he shouted like that and called her a cunt. *And* he'd took Storme out without a coat. He never noticed the weather himself. He wore the same clothes all year. Leather jacket and jeans. He even wore them in that heatwave when there was a hosepipe ban.

He'd got a visiting order to see Bilko in prison. He'd be in Veronica's café, 'Until half-past one,' he'd said.

'And I ain't takin' Storme in the nick,' he'd shouted. 'So get your arse down ere, cunt.'

They'd arranged that morning that he'd look after Storme while she went to the social to see about getting a loan for a new bed. The bed she shared with Crackle was so old the springs had come through the mattress. When the phone rang at twenty-five minutes to two, she'd dreaded answering it.

'What the fuck you doing *there*?' he'd said. 'You should be *here*, cunt.'

Visiting Bilko was the highlight of Crackle's life. He loved Bilko. At the end of each visit they clasped each other around the shoulders and said, 'I love you, man.' She'd seen it, it made her sick. He loved Bilko more than he loved her. She knew this. He wrote to him *every* week and used a first-class stamp. She couldn't read, but she'd looked at one of Crackle's letters, when he was out at night doing his business. His handwriting was crap.

It wasn't fair about the warrant. Why should she buy a telly licence? She never watched the BBC, 1 or 2. The BBC was for old people. It did her head in. She *couldn't* have gone to the court on June the 18th at eleven o'clock. It was the first anniversary of her mum's death. She had to go to the cemetery at ten o'clock, and meet her dad and put flowers on the grave. She couldn't be in two places at once, could she? Crackle had read the letter from the court out loud to her.

'Fined five hundred pounds in your absence.' So when the second bailiffs' letter came they'd had to move. It was a shame; she'd liked their old flat on the estate. It had central heating, not like this place, which had an icicle hanging from the bathroom window. It was disgusting how the council expected you to live. People on the estate took the piss out of the block their flat was in. 'Scumbag Towers' they called it. Though there was only three floors.

The flat was a right shit heap. She knew she ought to clean it up: do some washing and borrow the vacuum from her dad. Take the pots out of the slimy water in the sink, and take the rubbish downstairs. They'd have to do something about that mattress in Storme's cot which was so wet with piss it made your eyes run. She might start on it in the morning. Trouble was, Crackle didn't like her getting up early, and by the time they'd got dressed and ate something the day was gone. She was too tired to do anything at night. She kept Storme sitting in her pushchair most of the time, but she had to let her out some time, and then the little sod was all over the place, running about and touching things. She was a nightmare.

Tamara sidled up to the window and looked out. That warrant bloke was still there, waiting for her. Crackle would have to take Storme to the prison with him. She wouldn't play up. Not after this morning. She'd *had* to hit her to stop her *touching* things. She *had* to learn not to *touch* things. Crackle had given her big licks as well, which he was entitled to do. It was his CD player she'd touched and it was only a week old. It wasn't a *toy.* She had to *learn.* After she'd hit Storme hard on both hands, Crackle had said, 'Don't give her no breakfast either.' Then he'd put his face next to Storme's and *really* shouted, 'You touch the fucking knobs on my sounds again and I'll chop your fucking fingers off.' Then he'd took her out of her pushchair and given her big licks round the side of her head. She had to learn right from wrong. If she didn't she'd grow up bad, and Tamara and Crackle wanted the best for her.

Crackle was explaining his dilemma to Christopher. He had this mate, Bilko. He was in Welford Road on remand, innocent of course. The police didn't like him, that was all. His girlfriend, Tamara, should have been here to pick the kid up, but she'd let him down again. Thing was, he had a VO to visit Bilko.

Christopher frowned. 'VO?' he queried.

'Visiting order,' said Crackle, pleased to explain the jargon to the unshaven man with the hard dog.

Storme was picking at pieces of cold chip, and putting them into her small mouth.

'I can't take *her* with me, can I?' Crackle said, indicating Storme.

'No, you can't,' said Christopher, who couldn't bear the thought of the baby going back out into the cold without a coat. He looked outside. The wind was whipping at the clothing of the passers by. The sky was the colour of lead. The clouds bulged with snow.

'Leave her here, with me,' he said.

Crackle got to his feet. 'Yeah?'

Christopher put his hand on the pushchair.

'If Tamara don't come, I'll be back in an hour,' said Crackle, heading for the door. When he'd gone Christopher looked at the baby and stroked the dry hair back from her face.

'Hello, my chick,' he said. 'You're with me now. I'll look after you.'

Christopher took off his anorak and wrapped it around Storme until only her eyes and the top of her hair could be seen. He sat her back in the pushchair and looked for the restraining straps, but there were none.

'There, that's nice, isn't it? Warm as a bug eh? You're a good girl aren't you?'

He called the dog and it got to its feet. He pulled the pushchair backwards out of the café. A young man about to come in held the door open for him, nodding when Christopher thanked him. Storme closed her eyes briefly against the east wind and Christopher exhaled sharply as the cold struck at him through his plaid workman's shirt. They stopped at a traffic light and stood with other people, waiting to cross the road. Traffic thundered by. A woman carrying heavy shopping bags looked at the dog and moved away.

'We have to wait for the green man,' explained Christopher to Storme. 'There he is.' They crossed the road in the middle of the small crowd and walked along the pavement away from the prison.

Christopher stopped outside the Canine Defence League charity shop, and looked at the sparse display in the windows. There was a boxed set of tarnished fish knives, a mug decorated with the heads of Princess Margaret and Anthony Armstrong-Jones, a bright yellow teddy bear with glass eyes, and a tower of large boxed jigsaws against which somebody had leant a hand-written notice, 'Contents not checked'. A child's all-in-one snowsuit was draped across a boxed salad spinner. Christopher opened the door and asked an old woman, who was on her knees beside a black plastic bag full of old curtains, if he could bring the dog inside. She looked at the dog and smiled.

'Of course you can come in,' she said to the dog. 'We can't leave *you* outside can we? Not today.'

She got to her feet by bracing one hand against the shop counter. Christopher saw that her rings were almost lost inside the flesh of her swollen fingers. Storme watched as she crooned over the dog and stroked its hard flanks. Christopher unwrapped Storme from his anorak and sat her on the counter and asked the woman to fetch the snowsuit and the teddy bear from the window. When he gave Storme the bear to hold she took it without any sign of pleasure.

'They get so much nowadays,' said the woman disapprovingly.

Christopher struggled with the zip on the snowsuit. He carried Storme to the full-length mirror and stood her in front of her reflection. She stared gravely back at herself.

'You look beautiful, chicken,' said Christopher. He looked at the woman for confirmation, but she had evidently reached the age where she felt she had earned the right to speak her mind.

'I don't like this fashion for thin babies myself,' she said, 'but it's a good enough fit.'

When Christopher paid her he noticed that the till was almost empty.

In a shop called Shoes! Shoes! Shoes! he bought a tiny pair of red wellington boots. When she'd tried on the boots, Storme's socks had fallen off, and Christopher had been dismayed at the sight of her filthy feet and neglected toenails. He imagined her in his bath at home, pink and clean and splashing in the warm scented water. He would buy a bottle of that children's shampoo he had seen advertised on the television, the one that didn't sting their eyes. Storme walked carefully around the shop holding on to Christopher's finger. 'Boots,' said Christopher. 'Red boots.'

She stiffened slightly when he picked her up to place her back in the pushchair. Christopher guessed that she had enjoyed the novelty of walking in her new boots, but he was running out of time. It was time to take her back to the café, where one or possibly both of her parents were waiting to take her home.

Eight

On her way back to work Angela passed Woolworths, and was unable to resist going inside. She promenaded around the Pick 'N' Mix console twice before she made her selections. She noticed that there was something new since yesterday: cherry nougat. She would try that. She tore a plastic bag from its holder and began. A handful of chocolate limes, six chocolate brazils, a few nut crunch, four raspberry ruffles, a scoopful of liquorice torpedoes, a couple of cherry nougat, several sherbet lemons, half a scoop of chocolate raisins.

In the days immediately after she had left Christopher, she had turned to sweets and chocolate as other people turned to drink. She gorged herself with them in an effort to feel full again. She would wake in the night, in the bedsitting room she'd rented, and grope for the Mars bar that was waiting on the bedside table. She couldn't get out of her head the terrible noise he'd made when she'd told him she was leaving him. It was the saddest sound she'd ever heard.

She took nothing with her, apart from her clothes. Her friends thought she was mad to leave such a lovely man. But how could she have stayed? He rarely spoke and every time he looked at her she saw the accusation in his eyes.

The sides of her jaw ached, and a rush of saliva came into her mouth. She was hurrying now, desperate to get outside, to plunge her hand into the bag which she would conceal in her overcoat pocket. 'If I burn some extra calories tonight, I'll be all right,' she said to herself as she tore off another bag. She filled this second bag with assorted toffees (apart from the rum flavour, which she disliked), peppermint creams, fruit pastilles encrusted in sugar and, last of all, jelly babies in the sweet powder that she liked to lick off, leaving the babies clean and gleaming and new-born.

She waited until the queue had gone and then placed her bags on the scale. The pretty girl behind the cash till was wearing dark red lipstick. She opened her mouth to say, 'Five pounds, sixty-five pence,' and Angela saw with pleasure that there was a smear of lipstick on the girl's front teeth. It made her feel better about herself to see the imperfections of other women.

As soon as she got out of the shop she went to the litter bin in the street. She stood over it, unwrapping and discarding all the sweet wrappers and putting the sweets back in the bag. It was easier to eat them that way, and it meant that Gregory and the girls in the shop would find no evidence of her addiction.

As Christopher pushed Storme back towards the café, he glanced down and saw that the teddy bear he'd bought her had gone. It was too late now to retrace their steps and look for it. He'd already kept her out longer than he'd intended. If a stranger had been out with his own child for so long he'd have been frantic with worry.

'Are you all right, chick?' he said to her.

Storme threw her head back and looked up at him, and he wondered again what his own daughter would have looked like. He had two distinct pictures of girls in his mind. One was the passionate adolescent Catherine Earnshaw, with whom he had fallen in love during his reading of *Wuthering Heights* at the age of fourteen. The other was the golden-haired toddler, Eppie, in *Silas Marner*. He had pretended to Angela that he didn't care about the sex of their baby, but he had secretly hoped that it would be a girl.

It was seventeen years ago when Christopher had driven up the gravel drive and stopped his Bedford van outside the front entrance of The Elms Nursing Home. Before he could switch off the engine a woman in red-framed glasses came out and indicated irritably that he should have parked round the back. He blushed and in the slight confusion pressed his foot hard on the accelerator, the back wheels spun and sent the gravel flying. He looked in the rear-view mirror and saw that the woman looked angry now. He wanted to explain that he had not disturbed the gravel intentionally, but she had turned her back and was walking through the stone entrance of the building.

Christopher's life seemed to be dogged by these small misunderstandings. It was the same woman who told him where to find Angela. Though she refused to tell him why Angela was in the nursing home. She knew nothing about the phone call he'd had at work that morning.

'She's in the Lilac Room,' she said, jabbing in the air with a Bic pen. 'You're early,' she added. 'You'll have to wait.'

There was a smell in the building, a sticky red smell that made him feel slightly sick. He waited outside the Lilac Room until the minute hand on his watch touched half-past. Then he went in with the other subdued men, a legitimate visitor. There were eight beds in the room, all of them occupied. None of the women spoke, some lay on their sides, some on their backs. Angela was on her side, watching the door. When she saw him walk into the room, she pulled herself up on to her pillows. Christopher saw her glance at his work clothes and he wished he'd stopped off to change. He didn't know that his baby had been born and had died the night before. He'd thought that Angela was at a conference.

'What's wrong?' he said. He was shocked at her appearance. Her face was white and one eye was filled with blood.

She saw him looking and said, 'A blood vessel burst.'

'Is that why you're in here?' he said.

'No,' she said.

It hadn't been part of her plan that Christopher would ever come to this place. She had worked out what to tell him when she returned home: that she had suffered a miscarriage. But she had bled heavily and there had been trouble with the afterbirth. They had phoned Christopher as her next of kin.

'I lost the baby, Chris,' she said.

'No,' he said. 'That can't be right.'

'It happened last night.'

He looked down at the outline of her belly under the bedclothes.

'No,' he said.

There was still a slight swelling, he was sure of it.

A nurse came to the bedside and put a thermometer in her mouth, silencing her.

Her hands smoothed the stiff white sheet. He felt as if he were a stranger to her. The quiet presence of the other people in the room oppressed him and made him dumb. He sweated inside his work jacket: every word he had ever known had gone from his brain. He looked around the room. Was it a hospital? The walls were a shiny mauve, the linoleum floor was pitted with the heel marks of women's shoes. The hot air was heavy with the red smell. He touched Angela's hand, and stroked the eternity ring that should have had seven tiny diamonds in a claw setting. He'd bought it for her the day her pregnancy had been confirmed.

'You've lost a diamond,' he said. It came out sounding harsher than

46

he had intended. His tone was almost accusatory. Angela examined her ring.

'Sorry,' she said, mumbling through the thermometer.

'No, I didn't mean . . .'

The nurse came back, removed the thermometer and said, 'It's gone down. You could be going home tomorrow.'

'They might find the diamond,' he said. 'Shall I ask them to look?' He couldn't talk about the baby. If he did he might fall apart and never be whole again.

'Everything will have been cleaned by now,' she said. 'Tidied away, disposed of.' She was scornful of his ignorance of the procedures of the place.

'We'll get another diamond fitted, eh?' he said. 'We'll go into town on Saturday.'

'No,' she said. 'I don't want another diamond.'

They sat in silence for a moment, then she said, 'I'll never go through that again.' She looked at him with a stricken face. He felt an intense love for her. He leaned forward and put his arms around her. His coat flapped open and got in the way, its rough texture pressed against her face, and she pushed him away from her.

Five months before that day she had told him that she had missed her period and could be pregnant. He had immediately left the shabby top-floor flat they'd rented in a street of gloomy Victorian villas, and visited three off-licences before finding one that had proper champagne for sale. He had lied to her and said he was going out to buy cigarettes. She'd had a bath while he was out, and was drying her long black hair in front of the gas fire when he returned.

He placed the bottle of champagne on the coffee table and went into the small kitchen. Angela watched the condensation trickle over the Moët et Chandon label. She could hear him looking through the cupboard where they kept the glasses. She went to the kitchen door. He was polishing two glasses with a clean tea-towel. He was smiling to himself.

'Do you want a boy or a girl?' he said.

'For God's sake, Chris,' she said.

He handed her a glass of champagne.

'This is ridiculous. I've only missed a period.'

'You're pregnant, I know you are,' he insisted. 'You look different,' he added.

She glanced into the speckled mirror that hung over the sink where he shaved and she put on her morning make-up.

She hadn't had the heart that night to tell him that she didn't want a baby. She liked leaving the flat in the morning carrying her briefcase, and wearing her smart clothes. She didn't tell him that she almost despised the young mothers she passed at the school gate, with their pushchairs and their air of dependency, and their neglected appearance.

When the cork exploded from the bottle, it hit the cracked ceiling and flakes of plaster floated down on to their heads. Christopher filled the glasses and laughed. 'We'll have to move from here, we can't bring a baby up in the red-light district can we?' A woman with a grotesquely over-made-up face had recently moved into the bottom flat with two noisy children. She solicited on the doorstep during school hours.

Angela and Christopher touched glasses and drank. The moment had passed when she felt she could be honest with him. She watched him as he smiled down into his glass. His thick fingers held the stem delicately. Later, in bed, he asked her if he could hold her belly. She had said yes, but as she felt his hand slide under her nightgown and come to rest on her warm abdomen, she knew it wasn't her he was caressing. He made love to her with an intensity that frightened her. Afterwards she lay in the dark, and willed the blood to come between her thighs and stain the sheets.

The next day Christopher started to look for somewhere suitable to bring up their baby. Angela would be at home, of course, and they couldn't afford a second car, so things like schools, shops and bus stops would have to be within easy walking distance of their new house.

One day he was on his way to a hotel on the western outskirts of the city, where he had a contract to service all eighty-three of the in-room television sets, when he saw a 'For Sale' sign in the front garden of a semi-detached house. March sunshine gave the brickwork a pink glow that appealed to him. He stopped the van and opened a small waist-high gate, and walked up a path lined with grape hyacinth and narcissi. He lifted the brass flap of the letterbox and peered inside. There was a parquet floor in the hallway, and a child safety gate on the bottom of the stairs. He walked around the back. There was a long lawn and apple and pear trees.

The house was called Avalon. When Christopher arrived home that night he looked it up in *Brewer's Dictionary of Phrase and Fable* and found that Avalon was the Island of Blessed Souls. He knew there and then that he and Angela and their baby would live in this house.

Angela was three and a half months pregnant on the day they moved in. She walked through the empty rooms listlessly. He wouldn't let her carry any of the boxes or help him remove the furniture, even the small pieces, from the van.

Unknown to him, she had tried many times to rid herself of the child. She had sat in baths of water so hot that her legs and thighs had turned scarlet. She had once drunk half a bottle of gin and made herself so ill that Christopher, returning from work, had called the doctor. She had bought laxatives from the chemist and attempted to purge the baby out of her, but it clung to her like a limpet.

Nine

'Thought you weren't coming back,' said Crackle, when Christopher wheeled Storme up to the table where he and a white-faced girl were sitting crouched over an ashtray. He unfastened the dog's lead from the handle of the pushchair.

'What's she wearing?' said the girl, accusingly, looking at the snowsuit.

'It's only second-hand,' said Christopher. Storme drummed her feet in their new boots against the footrest of the pushchair. She looked up at her mother.

'The boots are new,' Christopher said.

'She's got shoes, *and* a coat at home,' said Tamara defensively.

She's done everything she can to make herself unattractive, repulsive even, thought Christopher, looking at Tamara's spiky black crew cut. There was a ring in her left nostril, another pierced her thin upper lip. Her eyes were lined, Cleopatra-like, in black paint. She wore an outsize black baggy sweater that came down to her knees, black jeans and brown boots that looked ridiculously big for her. Like Crackle she wore a ring on each finger. Christopher noticed with distaste that Crackle and Tamara's rings were identical.

'I'd give *owt* for a dog like that,' said Crackle. 'What do you think, Tam?'

'Yeah, it's nice,' said Tamara.

'I might buy you one for Christmas,' said Crackle, 'play your cards right.'

'No,' said Tamara. 'I want a rottie – the devil's dog.'

Her little girl's voice was at odds with the things she was saying.

'No, you can't keep a rottie in a flat,' said Crackle.

She whined, 'I know lots of people who've got them in flats.'

'Rottweilers need a lot of exercise,' said Christopher. He didn't want them to get a Rottweiler, or any kind of dog.

Christopher crouched down in front of Storme.

'Goodbye then, Storme,' he said.

Storme pulled on the toes of her red boots.

'Boots, yes,' said Christopher. He called the dog and left the café without looking back at her. He wanted to care for Storme always. To feed her, and keep her close, and teach her things.

As he walked away from the city he pointed out to the dog that the snow was melting and that the gutters were full of water. People passed him on the pavement, but nobody seemed to think him peculiar for talking to his dog. Before he turned into the Close where he lived he told the dog that he would find a way of caring for Storme; 'putting colour in her cheeks', he said.

He had grown up with cinema advertisements featuring children with plump red cheeks and fitted coats with velvet Peter Pan collars. He imagined Storme aged three, running towards him wearing such a coat. The picture was so vivid that he could see the rows of stitching on the collar and the white socks and patent leather Start-Rite shoes with a silver buckle she wore. The ribbon in her hair was red, made of taffeta. He would make sure that she always wore proper fitting shoes, and that she went to the dentist every six months. She would have ballet lessons and a library ticket, and she would live in the country where it was safe. Her toenails would be cut straight across with scissors bought especially for the task. He would read her bedtime stories, *Winnie the Pooh* and *The Little Prince*, and protect her from the violence and anxieties of the television news. She would sleep in clean sheets, in a warm room with sufficient ventilation.

There would be an alphabet frieze running around her room, so that she could lie in her little bed and learn her letters in dreamy comfort. There would be a brown egg at breakfast, and yellow butter and bread cut with a knife. There would be a tablecloth and a wooden chair with a cushion so that she could reach the table. There would be hollyhocks in the garden. He would give her a small watering can. In the winter he would roast chestnuts for her on the log fire and teach her the old nursery rhymes. He would cherish her and keep her in this fictitious childhood world until she was grown, and only then would he let her go.

Ten

As Angela drove around the multi-storey carpark following the exit signs, Catherine appeared beside her. Angela told her about the extra-ordinary meeting she'd had at lunchtime with Christopher Moore.

'He just turned up?' Catherine was amazed. 'What does he look like?'

'Well, you wouldn't want him to come to a parents' evening, not looking like he did today.'

Catherine asked, 'Does he know about me?'

'Catherine, *you* are all we talked about,' said Angela. 'You and his dog. He wanted to know if you were alive.'

'What did you tell him?'

'I told him the truth. I told him that you were dead.'

They both laughed, and Angela took her eyes off the road for a moment to glance at her impossibly perfect, beautiful, black-haired, laughing daughter.

'I got a hundred per cent in my mock A's, Mum,' said Catherine, smiling and showing her dazzling teeth. Angela glowed with maternal pride as she stopped at the barrier and handed her ticket to the gloomy carpark man who sat in his little cubicle, listening to a Radio One traffic report. 'You're very young, but with your IQ and exam results you ought to try for Oxford next year,' Angela said to Catherine.

'Oxford?' repeated the carpark man.

'I was talking to my daughter,' said Angela. The man looked into the car. It was empty, apart from the fat woman behind the wheel.

Her talking to herself was nothing new to him; he'd seen all sorts of mad behaviour taking place in cars. Have a butchers at her now. She's crying her eyes out! She's had to pull over. She's dropped her head on the steering wheel and sounded the horn. She's looking for a tissue, can't find one. Ugh! she's blowing her nose on her skirt. A respectable-looking woman like her. The public never failed to amaze him. He'd often thought of writing it all down. He could fill a notebook a day.

Angela couldn't stop the water from pouring down her face just as the amniotic fluid had trickled from her womb, before Catherine had been born. They had given her prostaglandin intravenously in a drip inserted into the back of her wrist. She had not been able to watch while it had been inserted. She had looked at the glossy white walls and the metal shelves stacked with sterile packs and stainless steel instruments. There had been a haze of fear in her eyes as she had walked into the room, and climbed on to a high trolley, and this had prevented her from seeing where she was at first.

She had not remembered the doctor's name. She could not properly understand his heavily accented English. He grew impatient with repeating himself to her, and looked frequently at his watch, as though he had a more important appointment elsewhere.

'Why did you not have an abortion earlier?' he said to her as he straightened up after examining her cervix.

'I'm sorry, what did you say?'

'Why not *earlier*?' he said, raising his voice.

'Earlier?'

'A termination, before twenty-seven weeks. That is usual.'

'My fiancé wanted the baby,' she said.

'And is he still wanting the baby?' The doctor lifted the white surgical gown she wore, and palpated her abdomen with cold brown hands. Angela imagined the baby cowering away through the layers of skin, fat muscle, and fluid, from the roughness of his touch.

'Yes, he still wants the baby.'

'So you are defying him?'

'Sorry, what did . . .'

'You are aborting this baby against his will?'

'Yes,' she said.

'You know you will go into labour, and that we cannot predict how long your labour will last?'

'Yes, I understand that.' She had spoken to a counsellor and this kindly woman had explained that a late-term abortion was 'particularly upsetting'. Angela had read in a gynaecological text book that labour would be painful and was often protracted. She looked at the counsellor's floral print dress, and tried to put a name to the flowers. Freesias? Aquilegia? She looked up and heard her saying, '. . . psychological problems.'

Angela had wanted to shout at the woman. I don't think you can properly understand how much I want to get rid of this baby. It is an alien inside me. It has filled my belly and my head. It has turned me into an animal with an animal's responses. It is a loathsome parasite, feeding off me. Would you have me welcome a *tapeworm* into the world? I want all traces of it cleared out of my body. I will excavate the thing, by hook or indeed by crook. If the labour takes a year, and the pain makes me scream like an animal in a trap, I don't care. I will face it with fortitude. When the invader has gone, I will reconvene: I will gather together the threads of my old life, and I will forgive myself and eventually forget.

The kindly woman in the floral dress said, 'Do you have any questions, Angela?'

'Yes,' said Angela. 'How soon can you fit me in?'

Eleven

Gregory was waiting impatiently for Angela to come home. He'd bought a £2.99 bag of Realwood logs from the garage on his way back. When he heard her key in the door he would put a match to the kindling in the hearth. He lit a cigarette, a low-tar brand, called Ultra Low. He took the cigarette from a zippo chromium case he'd received on his eighteenth birthday from his girlfriend at the time. 'Love always, Elaine.' He rubbed the inscription with his thumb. On 30.7.76 Elaine had informed him that she had been in love with her dentist for over a year and she could 'no longer live a lie'. The dentist, Mr Chan, was unaware that he was the object of Elaine's love, and eventually was forced to take an injunction out to keep Elaine away from his surgery.

Gregory thought that he should stop using the cigarette case. For twenty years it had been a constant reminder to him that before Angela he had always seemed to end up with difficult, neurotic women. The type who cried easily and wore unflattering clothes that were five years behind in fashion. These women had looked unfashionable even *without* their clothes. He wondered why even their naked bodies had looked second-hand. He wasn't what women called 'a catch'. He knew that. But he was a damned sight better looking than *most* of the husbands and partners he saw about. And better educated (two A levels) and he'd almost completed a degree at Loughborough University in Leisure Management. In a moment of uncertainty he'd once done a quiz in the *Sunday Times* and had scored just enough points, forty-five, to categorise himself as middle-middle-class. He'd got five of those points because as a young man he'd played rugby and tennis at club level, before persistent cartilage problems had forced him to stop.

Sometimes he wondered if he was performing the sex act correctly. None of them had complained, but he had to admit that not one of them had shown the wild abandonment that women on the cinema screen went in for. He had tried to arouse them by showing them drawings from *The Joy of Sex* but he couldn't recall a single ex-girlfriend who had bitten a pillow or thrashed her head from side to side. He was always scrupulous about their mutual sexual hygiene but, after having sex with him, few of them ever wanted to see him again.

It was so unfair. He'd go to enormous trouble: he could only bring them to the house on Tuesday nights when his mother went to rehearsals at the local dramatic society. After she'd gone he would pick the girl up from her home and drive her back to his mother's house, light the gas fire in the lounge, adjust the lighting, lay a towel on the hearth rug, and put 'Bolero' on the record player. Making love by firelight should have been a magical experience, but most of the girls had been unable to relax; some had been frightened; some had cried and had wanted to go home.

Angela had broken this unhappy pattern. She was a looker. She was interested in world affairs. Their fathers had both been members of the Lions Club of Great Britain. She was an older woman. She was sexually experienced. He'd asked her to marry him in the carpark of a country pub on their third date. They'd been standing watching the sun setting between two tall conifers and Angela's face was suffused by the fading pink light. He had driven them back to town without once exceeding the speed limit. A queue of cars had built up behind them. Angela's right hand had stroked his left thigh. This was the most physically intimate they had been so far. They had gone back to Angela's bedsit for sex. She seemed to be desperate for him. He had phoned his mother to tell her that he wouldn't be home that night, he was staying with a friend from the rugby club. His mother had laughed indulgently down the phone.

'You *men*,' she'd said. Though it was only eleven o'clock at night. Gregory had meant to remind his mother to lock the front door, but he had been unable to speak. Something had been put into his mouth; it was one of Angela's nipples.

Gregory hadn't wanted to spend his working life surrounded by napery, but when his father, sole proprietor of Lowood's Linens, had dropped dead at work at the age of fifty-three, the family business had settled itself on his reluctant twenty-one-year-old shoulders. He had never succeeded in shrugging it off. Initially he'd agreed to it to please his mother, who had been hysterical at the graveside, and had implored him in the funeral car to carry on where his father had so suddenly broken off. He would have agreed to anything during that terrible journey. Anything to shut her up, to stop that embarrassing wet-mouthed grief, and those awful unfeminine out-of-control grunting noises she was making in the back of her throat. His mother had always been such a quiet woman. The drive back from the church-yard to the family house became a fifteen-miles-an-hour nightmare. As the black car passed Lowood's Linens his mother began screaming, 'How can I live without him?' He had wanted to slide the glass panel aside and ask the driver of the car to put his foot down, but Lydia, his older sister, had restrained him.

Within three years his mother had died, leaving Gregory the large Edwardian house in the comfortable suburbs to the south of the city and rooms full of Jacobean-style dark furniture. Lydia had wanted the dining table and eight chairs. There had been a quarrel which turned into a feud, he hadn't seen her for sixteen years. Gregory was now thirty-nine and was still surrounded by tablecloths and napkins, in the tiny shop, opposite the noisy market place. After a lot of agonised indecision, he had diversified into bed linen, and expanded into the shop next door, but napery was still his speciality. There was nothing Gregory didn't know about the trade. The shelves of the shop were stacked to the ceiling with every conceivable fabric and pattern of tablecloth and napkin.

His father had been a *character*; he had been well known in the town for his wit and bonhomie, and his capacity for strong drink. A glam-orous woman, a stranger, had turned up, uninvited, to his funeral. Gregory also wanted to be thought of as a character. He tried to make himself more interesting by wearing a three-piece suit and a bow tie to work. There was always a fresh flower in the button-hole of his coat. For a time he had taken to buying the *Daily Telegraph*. He had enjoyed sitting on his high stool next to the till, flapping and cracking the large broadsheet pages into order; but he had eventually tired of what he called, 'the smart-alecky' writing, and had gone back to the *Daily Mail*, which was more manageable, on many levels.

On Wednesdays, Fridays and Saturdays he employed a young woman, to help in the shop. She was black, had three school-age children and was called Lynda. Gregory chose her *because* she was black. He thought it would make him seem advanced and daring. Lynda had not turned out to be as exotic as he had expected. She didn't laugh as easily as he would have liked or wear bright colours. She was efficient and honest and polite to the customers and within a few weeks she knew her way around the stock.

'But I could have had all that from a white woman,' he had once grumbled to Angela.

His regular customers now were mainly old women, to whom a tablecloth was still a household necessity, but Christmas brought all types. He could move a hundred tablecloths a day in the week before Christmas. His best line was a red cloth bordered with a Santa and reindeer design. He imported these from Portugal. He could fill in the customs and excise forms with his eyes closed.

Over the years, he had taken up many hobbies and pastimes. He had collected early English teaspoons. He had then become interested in genealogy, and had traced his Lowood ancestors back to the eighteenth century. Disappointingly, they had been tanners – the pariahs of a village in Norfolk, forbidden even to go to church because of the 'noxious odure' of their clothing. Gregory had also experimented constantly with his facial hair; a handlebar moustache, mutton-chop whiskers, a goatee, a bushy and a half-face beard, but somehow or other his quest for the public label, that of being a 'character', continued to be fruitless.

He fancied himself as a bit of a scribbler and had once embarked on writing a heavily researched science fiction story about a crew of women astronauts attempting to land on Saturn, but by the nineteenth page they'd already reached Saturn and he hadn't known what to do with them after that, so he'd abandoned the book.

What he wanted was to walk into a country pub and hear a shout go up: 'What's your poison, old boy?' He wanted to be part of a VAT-grumbling, joke-cracking, heavy-drinking crowd of small businessmen like himself. He wanted to be a man. He had no real interest in football, except on the rare occasions when his local team did well, but recently he had started to read the sports pages in the newspapers and to study the football league tables.

He'd often thought about selling the shops and buying a country pub. He would supply faggots and peas after the darts matches, and encourage his regulars, his friends, to keep their personal tankards hanging up over the bar. He'd mentioned this idea to Angela, but she'd said, 'Quite honestly Gregory, I'd sooner sell my body in Wolver-hampton, than run a country pub.'

Twelve

Angela fumbled at the bottom of her handbag for her keys. Her fingers touched a clothes peg, then a tampon. She could have rung the door-bell. Gregory's car was parked in the driveway, but she had grown to hate the way he opened the door to her when she'd forgotten her key on these occasions; as though she were not his wife, but a stranger who had interrupted him in some important task. He never mislaid his keys, he kept them on a long key-chain which he attached to a belt loop on his trousers. There were seventeen keys on Gregory's bunch. They bulged in his right-hand trouser pocket.

When Gregory opened the front door, he found his wife on her hands and knees on the doorstep, crouched over the contents of her handbag.

Angela smelt wood-smoke in the hall-way and knew that she was in for at least an hour and a half of sexual activity in front of the log fire in the living room. When she had gathered her things together and thrown them into her handbag, he extended his hand and pulled her to her feet. They went into the kitchen and unpacked the plastic grocery bags in silence. When everything was in its proper place, Gregory said, 'Shall we go and sit by the fire?' It was what he always said.

She went into the living room with him and sat down on the brown leather sofa. He put his arm around her neck and pulled her towards him. He pecked at her with his thin lips. His moustache felt like a small animal grazing on her mouth. He got up and crossed to the switch by the door and dimmed the wall lights. Then he went back to her and kissed her more ardently. He then pulled her down on to the towel which he had laid over the Chinese patterned hearth rug in front of the fire. He removed her outsize clothes and folded them carefully and laid them in a mounting heap on the carpet.

Angela closed her eyes and thought about the delicious sex she had once enjoyed with Christopher Moore in the sagging bed they had shared when they were young. They had devoted whole weekends to making each other happy. She could still smell the pungency of the sheets as she rammed them into the mouth of the industrial washing machine at the launderette on Monday evenings. Sometimes she had felt dizzy with remembered desire and had been obliged to leave the humidity and the swirling drums of clothes and go out into the night to cool off.

Gregory placed his jacket, trousers and tie on the wooden multi-purpose hanger he always used. Then hung it on the hook behind the door that he'd fixed there for the purpose. He removed his thermal vest, underpants and socks and placed them behind a cushion on the sofa. He went to the switch on the wall and turned the lights off. Then he bent over the fireplace and thrust a long copper poker with a jester's head, in between the smouldering logs. He needed flames: flickering firelight. Once, when drunk, he'd tried to explain why, but had only got as far as telling her about a camping trip with the scouts, before becoming incoherent.

'I'll fetch a firelighter,' he said, and slipped his bare feet into his brown felt slippers. Angela arranged herself as best she could into a fetching arrangement: one leg slung over the other, toes pointed. One hand supporting her stretch-marked breasts. Head thrown back so as to tauten her chins. He knelt down, she heard his knees crack, he leaned over her awkwardly and kissed her newly revealed neck. 'Wait for me,' he said, and crossed the lounge, hiding his genitals with one hand. After he'd closed the door, Angela let everything go and her body settled itself comfortably in the darkness.

When he returned a few moments later he was holding a single white firelighter ahead of him, like a baton. He looks like somebody about to run a relay race, thought Angela. And, as he crouched over the fire, breaking pieces of petroleum-soaked stick over the logs, he could indeed have been settling himself into the starting blocks waiting for the sound of the starting pistol. Once the fire was blazing he excused himself again, and went to the cloakroom where Angela listened to him washing his hands and brushing his nails.

Gregory had nothing to do with Angela's orgasm, twenty minutes later. It was entirely Christopher Moore's doing. It was the first time she had ever been unfaithful to Gregory, and she was surprised to find that she didn't feel at all guilty. She lay on her back and watched the colours in the fire and was just wondering how long it would be before Gregory reached his own climax, when an exploding spark from the fire fell on to Gregory's hairy back, and he leapt off her and yelped in pain, and flailed at his back with his right hand. His penis quickly lost height and size, until it resembled a one-eyed creature hiding in a cave. 'Should have put the fire-guard up,' he grumbled as he gathered his clothes together. Then, 'Aren't you getting up?'

'Not yet,' she said. 'It's lovely, just lying here.' He stood looking down at the full expanse of her. His hand was covering his genitals again. She didn't arrange her body in the customary way. She was fully conscious, but her body lay flat and totally relaxed, as though she had been anaesthetised for an imminent surgical operation.

When Gregory had pulled on his Y-fronts and left the room to make some tea, Catherine came and lay down beside her mother. She had to write an essay in German about Cologne cathedral and she was worried. Angela listened to her and told Catherine that if she got stuck she must bring the essay and they would work on it together. She kissed her daughter's beautiful face and squeezed her hand and said, 'You're my perfect, perfect dream girl.'

The door opened and Gregory came in carrying a tray on which were two glasses of Tia Maria and a Chinese rice bowl containing Marks and Spencer's prawn crackers.

'*Ich liebe dich*, Mum,' said Catherine, and was gone.

Lionel locked his bike in the shed at the bottom of his small garden. He'd forgotten his gloves and his hands were numb with cold and where he had gripped the handlebars. As he struggled to turn the key in the padlock, he looked down the garden to the terraced house where he could see his wife sitting behind the window in their living room, watching the nine o'clock news on the television. A picture of Nelson Mandela was showing on the screen and Lionel wondered if he was dead. He tapped on the window before opening the side door to the kitchen and his wife turned round and blew him a kiss through the glass. It was their evening ritual. As he passed through the kitchen, he saw his dinner on a film-wrapped plate, waiting by the microwave. As he ate it he would tell his wife, who was always eager for news, about his day in the booth of the multi-storey carpark. As he took his coat off, he decided that tonight's anecdote would be about the fat woman who talked to herself about her daughter.

Thirteen

It was in bed on a Sunday morning in June that Christopher first felt the baby moving inside Angela. He was lying half awake with one hand on her belly. At first he felt no more than a fluttering, as though a fledgling were practising bird-flight from the safety of the nest. Then there was a movement, a slight shifting of position. Christopher was fully awake now and he tried to wake Angela, but she turned her belly away from him. He got out of bed and came around to Angela's side. He peeled back the sheets and blankets and watched her belly. He loved the swelling of it, the recent definition of her womb. He held her belly with both hands and felt the child kick at the point where his thumbs were connected. He looked at the clock and noted the time: 8.13 a.m. He would remember that, he thought. Angela half woke and felt for the bed coverings, and Christopher pulled them over her and tucked them around her neck. He then went back to his side of the bed and lay down and wondered what it must be like to have a living thing inside you.

He called the child Catherine in his mind. He said it out loud. 'Catherine', then he said, again out loud, 'Catherine Moore'. He wanted her to have his surname. Angela stirred.

'What?' She opened her eyes.

'How about Catherine?' he said.

'Catherine?' She didn't understand, she didn't know a Catherine.

'For our *baby*. Catherine. I felt her move, Angie.'

She turned over and buried her head in the pillow. He shouldn't have named it, or felt it. It had been stirring inside her now for over a week. She hadn't told him because these new stirrings were disgusting to her. She felt as though she was being consumed by an alien force. One that was swallowing her up and making her invisible.

'How about William, if it's a boy?'

It was all he talked about lately. The baby.

She felt his hand sliding under her, then his left hand move over her back to link up with the right, and girdle her belly. She knew he was waiting for the baby to move again. He was as still as an angler waiting for a fish to bite. She got out of bed abruptly, breaking the circle of his arms, and went into the bathroom and stood under the shower. She washed her hair and shoulders and arms. She could not bring herself to touch her taut belly, or her blue-veined breasts, which had swollen so much that she no longer recognised them as her own. Under the noise of the rushing warm water she spoke to the baby. 'I don't want you, I don't want you, I don't want to be your mother.' Then she thumped the place on her belly where she had last felt movement. She thumped again and again until her fists ached and she was sure that the baby must be battered inside her. When she was towelling herself dry she avoided her belly and breasts, and let them dry naturally in the fresh warm air. She took her dressing gown off the hook on the bathroom door and put it on, and went downstairs to make the coffee.

While she waited for the percolator she listened to the floorboards creaking as Christopher moved around upstairs. She pictured his big sad face as he shaved and how very much sadder it would be when she told him that she no longer had his baby inside her. She laid four strips of raw bacon inside the grill pan, and put it under the grill. She watched the fat pour out and then frizzle and contract and harden, until each piece of bacon had changed its shape and texture and colour, and become something else.

When Christopher came into the kitchen, he was fully dressed; his hair was wet from the shower. He knew from the way Angela kept her back to him that something was wrong. The pregnancy book he had read had warned him that it was a time of 'hormonal changes' for Angela and he was to expect some 'mood swings'. The book asked him to be patient and loving. He went to the stove where she was spooning hot fat over uncooked egg yolks and put his arms around her belly. He was astonished when she spun around and pushed him away. He had never seen an expression of hatred on her face before. It made her ugly and it frightened him into silence.

He set the breakfast table carefully, with the blue and white striped crockery and the sleek cutlery they had bought for the new house in the Habitat shop that had recently opened in their town. He took a loaf out of the pine bread box and cut some slices of bread with the new Sabatier bread knife on the new ash bread board. The kitchen was full of sunlight, and he felt like a man in the Habitat catalogue until he noticed that the keen blade of the knife had sliced into the top of his thumb on his left hand and that crimson blood was bubbling out and dripping on to the last slice of bread in the small stack he'd cut.

He took his injury to show Angela, then to the sink where he watched his diluted blood sliding down the plughole. When she'd seen the blood flowing Angela had said, 'Lucky you.' Christopher was surprised. But of course, she must have meant to say, 'Unlucky you.' It was a slip of the tongue. He blamed the hormones. She would be perfectly all right when the baby was born. He wished Habitat was open on Sundays. It was time they sorted the spare room out and made a place for the baby, for Catherine or William. But preferably Catherine.

A week later she told him that she was going on a training course to learn about the computers that were going to revolutionise the travel industry. He believed her. But he said, 'Is it worth it for you, Angie? I mean, you'll be leaving your work soon, won't you, when the baby's here?'

Three days later he had helped her to pack a small overnight bag. She had removed two hundred pounds from her building society account and caught a train to Leamington Spa.

A mini-bus had picked her and six other women up from the station. They had not spoken to each other on the journey to the Elms. There was nothing to be said.

Fourteen

Storme woke up crying three times in the night. Twice she had woken Crackle. At four o'clock in the morning Tamara dragged herself out of bed again. She stood at the side of the cot, shivering, and trying to quieten her little daughter before she woke him up for the third time.

'Don't wake your dad, there's a good girl,' she implored in a whisper. But Storme struggled up through the stinking blankets and held her arms up imploringly. Tamara saw the tears on her face by the moonlight filtering through the dirty net curtain at the window. She pushed the little girl down and arranged the blankets on top of her as best she could in the dark. Storme cried out again, a cry so terrible and so piercing that Crackle woke and sat up in bed, an angry shape in the dark.

'What the *fuck*?'

'S'alright. Go back to sleep,' said Tamara to him. She put her hand over Storme's small mouth to try and stop the screams coming from her throat. But when she took her hand away the sound of Storme's misery filled the room and caused Crackle to leap out of bed and run to the cot and grab Storme by the front of her damp pyjamas. He held her level to his face and shook her, using her body as punctuation for his words.

'Shut, the, fuck, up. *Shut it!*'

Tamara was so afraid of his anger, she thought that her heart would burst through her chest.

'Perhaps she's poorly. I'll take her in the living room,' she said, trying to wrestle the baby away from him. The screaming was more than she could bear.

'There's nowt wrong with her, she's just playing up,' he said, and he threw the little child on to the bed face down and punched her in the small of her back.

She cried even louder. He picked her up by her shoulders and shook her violently, trying to stop the noise that she was making. Her head cracked against the wall above the bed and she stopped crying.

'See,' said Crackle, handing Tamara the damp whimpering body, 'she's gotta learn.'

Tamara laid her daughter on the cot mattress and covered her tenderly with the blankets. She was glad that it was dark and that she was unable to see the baby's face.

When she got into bed Crackle turned his back on her, but she could feel him breathing heavily from his exertions.

A feeling of dread kept her awake for a very long time, but eventually sleep overtook her and she half woke at dawn to find Crackle holding her belly, just as he had done when the baby had been inside her. It had been a good time. Crackle had insisted that she should attend every pre-natal appointment and had gone along with her. He kept the appointment card inside his wallet. He had punished her if she forgot to take her iron tablets. His face had been wet with tears when he had seen Storme lying on Tamara's belly, still attached to the milky cord. He had rung Bilko to tell him the glad news.

'I'm telling you Bilko, it's a fuckin' *miracle*,' he had said into the pay phone at the end of the gleaming corridor.

Tamara had stayed in the maternity hospital for three days. She was the only woman in the ward not to have a bouquet of flowers from her partner on her bedside locker. Crackle didn't believe in flowers. She pretended not to mind, but on the third night she pressed her face into the hospital pillowslip marked NHS in huge block letters, and cried. In the morning the pillow was stained with the black eye-liner and the make-up that Crackle thought was part of her face: he had never, to her knowledge, seen her without it.

Bilko drove the family back to their flat with great care; like a man with a fragile and precious cargo. Crackle sat in the front passenger seat jigging about excitedly, turning back occasionally to look at Storme, who lay asleep in Tamara's arms. Bilko's huge black face filled the driving mirror. He was a father himself. He knew that once the initial excitement of fatherhood was over Crackle would be looking for something else to fill his long workless days and nights. It was Crackle who had carried Storme over the splintered threshold of the flat. After the antiseptic sterility of the hospital, the smell in the flat made Tamara gag, but within a few hours she had accepted it again as being normal.

The morning after that terrible night Tamara stood over the cot, looking down at Storme. She looked different, thought Tamara. She was floppy and her eyes looked strange; as if they'd been replaced in the night by those of an alien baby. She carried Storme into the living room and switched on the fan heater. She couldn't wake her up, not properly.

She sat down on the decrepit sofa that the previous tenants had discarded. She rocked Storme in her arms until the room had warmed up, and then she took the baby's clothes off. She was shocked when she saw the bruise on her back. It was the same colour as the spring cabbage her mother used to cook in the happy days. Tamara knew that nobody in authority must see the bruise, or the sores on the baby's bottom that bled when she took off the sodden disposable nappy. She had a feeling that everything had gone too far, and that nothing would be the same ever again.

She wished that her mother was still alive. She would have known what to do. Tamara closed her eyes and remembered Snow White and a flock of bluebirds cleaning up the seven dwarfs' cottage in the woods. They would come to her council flat and do the same for her. They would put all the rubbish that had piled up under the sink into black plastic bags. Then they'd collect the used dirty pots that covered most surfaces in the flat and Snow White would soak them in hot water in the sink. Then the bluebirds would pick up the dirty clothes from the floors with their beaks and place them in bags, ready to be washed. Snow White would empty the ashtrays and scour the bathroom and toilet with Ajax, and sweep the accumulated debris from the floors. She'd clean the windows and ask the bluebirds to take down the ragged curtains and fly away with them. Then she'd sing that song and go round with a duster and Mr Sheen. Tamara opened her eyes and was almost surprised to find that Snow White and the bluebirds had not visited her, and that things were exactly the same.

Tamara couldn't imagine what her mother would have said or done if she had seen what had happened to Storme's body. Tamara hoped that her mother wasn't looking down from heaven at herself and Storme sitting on the sofa. She closed her eyes at the thought and kissed the top of the baby's head, softly so as not to wake her. It would be awful if she started to cry and woke Crackle. He was one of those people who needed his sleep. She would just have to sit quietly with the baby until he woke and shouted through for his coffee. She hoped it wouldn't be long. She was a bit worried about the baby – she was breathing funny. Tamara stretched out her hand and grasped the cigarettes and matches from the armrest on the opposite end of the sofa. She lit a cigarette and kissed the baby's head again. Smoke drifted across Storme's face, making her cough, which Tamara took to be a good sign. It was the baby's normal cough. The one she'd had for months.

Fifteen

It was November 25th, and at 9 a.m. Christopher was meant to attend a Job Club. This appointment had been made on his behalf by the Department of Employment, who had said in a letter that they were 'concerned about his long period of unemployment'. Christopher didn't share their concern. He had long ago reconciled himself to never working again, not in electronics.

After his grandma had died, a ridiculous thing had happened to him. He'd gone to work one day, a week after the funeral, and had started to cry. A song playing on the radio in the workshop had triggered it off. A Buddy Holly song that had held no significance for him, or for his grandma. He'd gone into the tiny room where he did his paperwork, and had tried to control himself, but it was as though a dam had burst and the waters were washing him away. He saw the embarrassed faces of his employees watching him through the interior windows. Douglas, the foreman, had come into the room and patted him on the shoulder and had made him a cup of tea and offered to drive him home. But Christopher had sat there ignoring the ringing phone, letting the tea go cold. The heating had switched itself off at 7 p.m., and he was aware that the temperature had fallen, and that he was very cold, but he couldn't move out of his chair. He was pinned down by a sadness so profound that he thought it would suffocate him.

In the morning Douglas had come in early and found Christopher asleep with his head on his desk. He had woken him up gently, and Christopher had started crying again. Douglas had not known what to do, apart from offering Christopher his handkerchief. The other employees had turned up and were dismayed to find their boss, usually so confident and fearless, whimpering like a small child, afraid of the telephone and hanging on to Douglas's hand. It was Douglas's wife, Anne, who had diagnosed a nervous breakdown, later to be confirmed by Christopher's GP. Tranquillisers had reduced the misery, but when he returned to the workshop three months later, he found a chaos of unpaid bills, unpresented invoices and unfilled orders. His business, of which he was now sole owner, so painfully built up over fifteen years, had unravelled like a badly knitted cardigan. In the short time he had been absent, he felt that he'd been left behind by the electronics industry. After the business was wound up he joined a large firm in the city. He'd got it into his head that he wouldn't live for much longer. He knew there was no rational reason for these morbid thoughts: he was in good health, it was more a feeling that he had already run the full span and was coming to the end of his life.

He took the dog for a walk on the heath. The police had gone, leaving deep tyre tracks in the muddy ground and a litter of cigarette stubs. He looked down into the ditch where the bag had been. It was half full of melting snow water. When he was a boy he would have delighted in playing in such a place, wading in his wellingtons, building a small dam, sailing tiny ships made of acorn shells with a dried leaf for a sail.

The dog jumped into the ditch and ran along its length, churning the mud at the bottom. Christopher walked away quickly. He was anxious to be as far away as possible when the dog climbed out of the ditch and shook itself. He was wearing his best suit and his only decent overcoat. He waited at the side of the dual carriageway for the dog. The traffic was heavy now with people on their way to work. A car passed him, pipped its hooter, pulled in and parked a hundred or so yards ahead. It was a Volvo estate, its hazard lights were flashing. The driver's door opened and Angela got out and started to walk towards him. He walked to meet her.

'I thought it was you,' she said. 'Can I give you a lift?'

'I've got the dog with me,' he said. At that moment the dog emerged from the scrubland wagging its tail and bounded towards him. Angela was taken aback by how different Christopher looked from yesterday. He had shaved and brushed his hair. He looked good in the masculine clothes he was wearing.

'I dreamt about you last night,' Angela lied.

'We don't see each other for seventeen years, and then twice in two days,' said Christopher. He bent down to click the lead on to the dog's collar so that she couldn't see from his face how happy he was.

'It *is* a strange coincidence,' she said. It was her second lie to him that day. The day before he had told her where he walked the dog in the morning. She had already driven around the perimeter of the heath seven times, in the hope that she would see him. Though she hadn't intended to stop the car, or to approach him directly.

'I'm going into town, but I'll have to take the dog home first,' he said. She was willing to put the wet and muddy-pawed dog in the back of the car. But the car was immaculate inside and Christopher insisted on walking the dog home. He gave her his address and she was sitting in the car brushing her hair outside his house when he and the dog turned the corner of the street.

'I love her,' he said to the dog. 'I still love her.'

The dog looked up at the sound of his voice. Then carried on sniffing excitedly at the pavement. It was always happy to return home after a walk.

She got out of the car, and smoothed her long overcoat down over her massive hips. She was wearing black suede ankle boots with delicate high heels. A black suede bag was slung over one shoulder. Her hair shone in the feeble morning sunlight. She had made up her face very carefully that morning, and had taken the cellophane wrapper off the Coco perfume she had bought in the duty-free on the Calais ferry a year ago. The nozzle was faulty and the perfume had poured down her neck in a stream, but she was glad now as she watched Christopher walk towards her. She wanted him to be intoxicated by her. To be enveloped and seduced by the smell of her.

Christopher hadn't wanted to show her around the house. He was ashamed of its masculine sparsity. He explained about the burglary and she sympathised. Her office had been burgled twice in the last year. They talked about insurance companies in his monastic bedroom. Christopher sat down on the double bed to change his shoes, and Angela caught a glimpse of herself in the wardrobe mirror. This was always a shock to her. She turned away quickly and went out on to the small landing. She looked into the other two bedrooms and was surprised to find that the walls were entirely lined with books. The shelves reached almost to the ceiling. Other books were stacked into cardboard boxes. One was full of Rupert annuals. She read the title of the top book through its polythene dust cover: *Rupert and the Snowman*. Christopher joined her at the threshold of the larger bedroom.

'So many books,' she said. She took a book out of its box. '*The History of Great Yarmouth*,' she laughed.

'It's what I do now. I read them and collect them.'

Both of them felt weak with desire. However, they were careful not to touch each other, and made subtle and deliberate manoeuvres to keep a space between them as they looked around the rest of the house.

Sixteen

The Job Club was held in a Portakabin situated in a carpark in the grounds of a defunct Victorian school, now converted into a skills training centre. The Portakabin next door was occupied by the Samaritans. Their tall radio mast swayed in the wind. Christopher watched it through the smeared window as he waited for other members of the Job Club to arrive. He had forgotten how to speak to people about unimportant things, so he kept his back to them.

At five past nine he heard a man's voice asking them to take a seat, and he turned around to see Barry Dearman standing beside a flow chart, with a black marker pen in his hand. Barry was smiling, showing his white crooked teeth. He told the assembled unemployed men and women that they almost certainly 'by now' suffered from low self-esteem, and that today's session would concentrate on getting their confidence back. He wrote 'SeLf-eSTeem' and 'COnFiDenCe' on the flow chart, in a mixture of upper- and lower-case letters, which irritated Christopher. A bald man sitting next to Christopher carefully copied 'self-esteem' and 'confidence' on the first page of a notebook which he took out of a W.H. Smith paper bag.

Barry then wrote 'Biography' on to the flow chart, then launched into an explanation of the word. He then handed out a sheet of thin A4 lined paper, so thin that Christopher could see his fingers through it when he took it from Barry's hand. 'When you've finished writing your biography, we're going to turn it into a CV,' said Barry; 'and some of you will get a chance to get on the computer and type it out, professional, like.' Thirty heads turned towards the lone computer which stood on a Formica table, trailing wires. The man next to Christopher wrote 'Computer' in his notebook.

Christopher wrote:

My name is Christopher Moore. I was born on July 20th, 1947. My parents were called Audrey and Harry. My father was a knitting machine engineer, and my mother worked in the hosiery making children's socks. However, due to circumstances, I lived with my grandparents from an early age. I attended Dovecote infant and junior schools and Ladymount Green Secondary School. My favourite subjects were English and History. In my last year I was in charge of the school library. I represented the school at table tennis. I left school when I was fifteen. I went to work in an electrical appliances shop, where I stayed for six years. During that time I learned to mend electrical appliances, including televisions, which not many people had then.

This was how I first met Angela. Her father came into the shop and asked if somebody would call at their house and have a look at their television, which had very poor picture quality. It took two buses to get there, they lived at Willoughby Harcourt, a small village. There was no such thing as the firm's van then, and anyway, I couldn't drive. The Carrs lived in a big house with a drive. I had to carry my toolbox all the way, and by the time I rang the bell I was glad to have arrived. Mrs Carr answered the door and showed me into a room she called the lounge. There were two bookcases, one on either side of the fireplace. The shelves were full of English classics: Dickens, Shakespeare, Waugh, Hardy: I'd heard of most of them. Televisions were big then, and this one (it was a Ferguson I think) stood in the corner, towering over all the other furniture. I'd taken the back off and was checking the wiring inside when Angela came in with a tray which held a cup of tea, a sugar bowl, and two digestives on a plate. Her first words to me were, 'My mother sent this.' She had a posh accent. My first words to her were, 'Thank you.' I think she was anxious to prove that she was intelligent, because she asked me a lot of questions about the science of television.

She had just taken an exam in physics, so I had to think very carefully before I answered her questions. She was eighteen, I was twenty-one. She was wearing a straight short dress. Her legs looked bright orange because of the stockings she was wearing and she wore white square-toed shoes. But it was her hair I liked. It was *so* black. I used to go bird-watching when I was a kid, and it was the same colour as a blackbird's wing. The tea went cold on the tray. I didn't dare risk making a slurping noise when I drank it. I asked her to turn the horizontal hold knob while I adjusted a few wires at the back, and after about fifteen minutes we got a perfect picture.

She was waiting to go to Leeds University. I have never loved anybody else. She didn't go. Her mother died after a long illness (cancer of the liver). She had to listen to her mother screaming with the pain. Then she had to stay at home and look after her father, who suffered from depression until he died, two years later. There was no money and Angela got a job in a travel agent's: her other A levels were in Spanish and German.

I next saw her in a jazz club. She was with a thin man with a beard. I hated him on sight. We were all on the dance floor. I asked her to dance. The bloke with the beard objected. I hated him so much that I hit him and he fell down.

Here Christopher asked for another piece of paper. Barry handed it to him begrudgingly, as if it were a sheet of gold leaf. Everyone else had long since finished writing.

It was the first time in my life that I had hit anybody before they hit me. Angela bent over her bearded friend and I was thrown out of the jazz club and told not to come back.

She came out with the bearded bloke. He tried to put his arm around her, but she threw it off. I knew that she had lost respect for him. I crossed the street and I said, 'Angela I love you.' I wasn't drunk. She started to cry. The bearded bloke hit me hard on the shoulder. I hit him back. Blood dripped from his nostrils.

'Don't, he's a poet!' Angela shouted. Her black hair fell across her face. I told her again that I loved her. She cried harder. The poet ran down the wet street and turned the corner. In those days there was nothing open in the town after 11 p.m. at night, so we sat in the bus station and talked until it got light. She told me about the deaths of her parents, and I told her that I loved her, repeatedly. I didn't touch her, though I wanted to. We had breakfast in the bus station café. It was two years before I saw her again at night school. Then another three before we lived together. I knew we would one day. Right from the moment we got the perfect picture together in the lounge at Willoughby Harcourt.

Barry walked around and gathered up the A4 sheets. He read them sitting on a chair by the computer. The unemployed adults watched him. 'Mr Moore,' he said, eventually. 'Could I have a word?'

Christopher had to stand in front of him. There was not a handy unoccupied chair. Barry craned his head and looked up into Christopher's face.

'Look, Chap,' he said. 'I haven't got the time to play silly buggers. I'm not here to read about Angela, or fucking liver cancer. I'm here to help you find a job!'

Christopher said, 'Don't say *fucking* in the same sentence you say *Angela*!' in a voice that reminded Barry of a British gangster film he'd seen in which softly spoken men did unspeakably cruel things to those who had offended them. Christopher realised that he didn't want to have any contact whatsoever with this man Barry. He knew he would never return to the Portakabin with the undulating floor. Or ever meet again the other job seekers. He decided to forfeit his job-seeker's allowance. He would live independently of the government and he would win Angela back. He slowed down as he passed the Samaritans' Portakabin, then decided that he didn't need them either. He walked in the direction of the city centre, increasing his pace as he neared the travel agency.

Seventeen

Tamara laid Storme down carefully on the sofa. She went into the bathroom to do her make-up. She examined her face in the magnifying mirror that was on the ledge propped up against the window. She wished that she looked older, like a woman instead of a girl, and that her face wasn't so thin. She would ask Crackle if she could grow her hair. It didn't suit her so short. She looked like those Bosnians she'd seen on the television. The hole in her nose where the ring had been inserted was sore. Yellow pus came out when she poked at it with a piece of tissue. She wetted the corner of a towel and dabbed it on to a sliver of soap that was stuck to the recess on the washbasin; then she wiped the towel under her eyes, removing the evidence of last night's mascara-stained tears. She opened the bottle of liquid eye-liner and, using a brush, drew two thick black lines around each eye. Then, using the little finger of her right hand, she dabbed the purple eye-shadow to the lids, mauve to the sockets, and pink to the expanse of shaven flesh under the eyebrows. She then spotted dots of pale liquid foundation over her face, and rubbed it in. Finally, she covered her lips with lipstick so dark that at first glance it appeared to be black.

The bath was full of dirty clothing. She sorted through it, looking for something to wear. She pulled out a pair of knickers that weren't too bad, but rejected the black jeans that no longer met round her waist. She found the red bra with the padded inserts that made her small breasts wobble slightly. In the past this effect had excited Crackle, but not lately. He'd gone off sex since he'd been on crack.

She tiptoed into the bedroom where Crackle was sleeping with one hand curled around his mouth. He looked so beautiful when he was sleeping; like a little boy. She drew the stained duvet over his thin back, covering the Satan tattoo and causing him to moan in his sleep, and move his head on the greasy pillow. She gazed down at him, enchanted by his long black eyelashes and his face that was prettier than hers when he smiled. She picked up from the floor some leggings and the baggy black sweater she'd been wearing since the weather turned cold, and put them on. As she crept back out, she saw the little red boots in a tangle of blankets at the foot of the cot. She searched through various piles of dirty clothing for something decent for Storme to wear. Something was telling her to take Storme to the doctor's. She looked at her watch, it was eleven – too late for morning surgery. She would have to wait now until four.

She found a pink stretch babygrow. It had been in the washing pile for a week, but after she'd scraped a patch of sick from around the neck with a long black varnished fingernail it didn't look too bad. She took a disposable nappy from the packet and began to dress Storme for her visit to the doctor. The baby slept throughout, which worried Tamara. When she was dressed, Tamara brought the towel with the wet corner from the bathroom and washed her daughter's face and hands. She noticed that the child's fingernails were rimmed with black, so she bit the end of a matchstick into a point, and used it to ease the greasy dirt from beneath each small nail. The fan heater stopped and the overhead light went out, which meant the electricity had gone. She hadn't got a card to insert into the meter. The room quickly grew cold, so Tamara covered herself and Storme with her red cloth coat that she wouldn't be seen dead in now, and they waited for Crackle, provider of money and electricity, to wake up.

When he shouted for his coffee, Tamara glanced at the Mickey Mouse clock that stood on top of the television – 12.15. She unwrapped herself from the coat and went through into the bedroom, taking Storme with her. He was lying on his back, smoking his first cigarette of the day – the one he enjoyed most. The ashtray on the floor next to the bed held a mound of ash and brown speckled filter tips. 'What's up?' he said, when he saw her face.

'She's not very well,' she said, sitting beside him on the bed, causing the blankets to tighten around him, outlining his thin body. He shifted irritably.

'What's up with her?' he said, flicking ash in the direction of the ashtray.

'She won't wake up properly,' she said. 'An' she's got a bruise.'

She undid the poppers on Storme's babygrow and showed him.

'Fuckin' hell,' he said, when he saw its green vividness. 'How did she do that?' he said, looking into Tamara's black-rimmed eyes. She looked back at him. It was like looking at herself. They were like twins, except that Crackle was clever, so clever that his teachers at school couldn't teach him anything. She loved him. They had married each other in the middle of a wood at midnight in September, on Friday the 13th. Crackle had said that the devil would be their witness. They had drunk two cans of Special Brew each, and dropped some Es and Crackle had fucked her up against a tree, and afterwards he had said they would be together for ever.

'How did she do it, Tamara?' he repeated.

'She done it falling out of her cot,' she said, and started to refasten the poppers. 'I'll tell the doctor that, shall I, this afternoon?'

'Yeah, tell him that, it's only the truth,' he said. 'Tell him the truth. Honesty's the best policy,' he said, recalling something somebody had once said to him. A teacher at school probably, or a solicitor, one of those stupid fuckers who believed it, anyway.

He got dressed and went out and bought an electric card. As good as gold, thought Tamara. He came back with a packet of Jaffa cakes, and they ate them, and drank Nescafé, and smoked cigarettes and watched a film about the olden days until it was time for afternoon surgery. Storme didn't wake up, her breath now came in a series of little gasps. Tamara tried her with a bottle of warm milk at half-past two, but she wouldn't take it.

'Stubborn in't she?' said Crackle affectionately.

'She takes after you,' said Tamara, and she stroked his bristly hair with a loving hand. Together they zipped Storme into the snowsuit that Christopher had bought the day before. They each took one of the little red boots and pushed them on to her feet. Crackle lowered her gently into her pushchair and they left the flat and carried her between them down the three flights of stone steps, as though they were children playing Mummies and Daddies. As they went out into the street snow was falling. Crackle took a delight in pushing the pushchair through the virgin snow on the pavement. Tamara laughed out loud as she tried to fit her own feet into his fresh snowy footprints. When the surgery came into sight Crackle said, 'What time did she fall out her cot, Tam?'

'Last night; I don't know what time,' she replied, not looking at him.

'About midnight, weren't it?' he said, pulling her round to face him. In the fading light her face was eyes and mouth only. He kissed her black lips and thrust his tongue between them, possessing her on the pavement as thoroughly as if they were alone, in the dirty bed, at home.

The doctor's receptionist recognised immediately that Storme was very ill, and ushered Crackle and Tamara through the waiting room with its silent crowd of patients and into the doctor's surgery. Dr Indu, a tiny Asian woman, asked Tamara to undress Storme. The doctor's thin hands felt the swelling on the back of the baby's head first, then she lifted the vest and saw the turquoise bruise on her back.

'What has happened to her?' she said.

'She fell out her cot, last night, about midnight,' said Tamara, looking at Crackle.

'Why didn't you call me out?' said the doctor, feeling the baby's pulse.

'We thought she would be all right,' said Crackle.

The doctor picked up the internal telephone and said, 'Mrs Parker, ring for an ambulance and put a call out also for Mr Parker-Wright at casualty.' When she had finished examining the baby's dirty body, the doctor could hardly bring herself to look at the baby's parents, with their sour-smelling black clothes, and their ridiculous barbaric ornaments. But she said, as evenly as she could, 'Mr Parker-Wright is a consultant paediatrician. Your baby is very ill.' She said again, 'Why didn't you call me?'

'She just went back to sleep,' said Crackle. 'Like she is now.'

'She is not *sleeping*, she is in a coma! Can't you tell the difference?'

The doctor was angry and sick of talking to such low-class people. They were as ignorant, despite their advantages, as the peasants she had cared for in the Indian villages where she had been sent after completing her training.

The receptionist came in and handed the doctor Storme's medical notes. The doctor read through quickly. Her colleague in the group practice, Andrew Wilson, had written three months before: 'The child shows signs of neglect, she is failing to thrive.'

'You have not brought her for her inoculations,' she said when she looked up.

'I kept getting the days wrong,' said Tamara.

They heard the ambulance coming towards the surgery. The doctor took a blanket from the examination couch and wrapped Storme up against the cold air outside. Crackle lit a cigarette when they were outside on the pavement. He dragged greedily on it, then threw it down regretfully before climbing into the back of the ambulance with Tamara. The doctor held Storme tightly to her as they rode through the streets towards the hospital. Tamara could not take her eyes off the red boots dangling from beneath the blanket. They could have been worn by a puppet whose strings had been cut.

Eighteen

When Angela saw Christopher push the agency door open she got up quickly from her computer, which was displaying a list of charter flights to Tenerife, and went into the back. She needed a few moments to compose herself. She both resented and welcomed his presence at her workplace. She combed through her hair with her fingers and smoothed her jacket over her hips: it was an habitual gesture.

He would always be able to find her here, she thought. From nine until five-thirty, six days a week. And if she changed her job, or moved to another country he would track her down eventually, she knew that. She felt an emotion she couldn't identify immediately, a mixture of excitement and fear – a fairground emotion. She saw herself, the timid child, being urged on to the big wheel by her mother, who did not want to ride in the lucent night air with a stranger beside her in the swaying carriage.

She came back into the shop. When she saw his smiling face she was lost. Who else would ever be so happy to see her? Snowflakes were melting into his hair. She looked away from him to the windows and saw that the street outside had been transformed from grey to mellow white. The flakes were so fat that it was possible to follow their individual progress before they settled with the uncountable millions on the pavement. They watched the snow fall in silence for a while, then Christopher said, 'I can't stop thinking about you,' as though he were explaining to her the nature of an illness he was suffering from. Angela glanced towards her colleagues, but they were busy with customers and hadn't heard his oblique declaration of love. His coat was open, he had unfastened the top button of his shirt and loosened his tie. She wanted to slip her hand inside his shirt and stroke the back of his neck as she had often done before, when they were young. It had been a prelude to making love. One of the many signals between them. She became aware of her nipples inside the utilitarian cotton bra she had to wear now. She was close enough to him to feel his breath on her face. She said softly, 'I'll get my coat,' and went back behind the counter. She told Lisa, Claire and Andrea that she had been called away to attend to urgent family business. After she had left the shop her colleagues speculated on the nature of the 'family business'. They decided that it would have to be an imminent or sudden death. Angela was always so punctilious about the hours she worked; she never took advantage of her seniority.

Christopher stood at the rack where the brochures were displayed, and read about holidays where it was possible to combine both the wedding *and* the honeymoon. There were photographs of attractive couples in wedding clothes posing against a tropical background of setting sun and palm trees. After two minutes, as arranged, he replaced the brochure on the rack and left the shop. They met a quarter of a mile away on the stinking stairs of the multi-storey carpark, but it was not until they got into the car that they took each other into their arms and smelt the breath and the skin of each other, and tasted the saliva and felt the scrape of eyelashes against their faces, and heard the wordless sounds of desire and longing that passed between them.

In his ticket booth, Lionel watched on a closed-circuit TV camera as the Fat Woman and the Tall Man embraced in the front seats of the Volvo. He knew they weren't man and wife. He'd seen the Fat Woman's husband, he was a small bloke with a moustache who never said please or thank you when Lionel gave him his change.

When Angela eventually drove up to the booth and handed Lionel her ticket, he spoke to her.

'Leaving work early today, madam?' he said.

'No,' she said. 'It's my day off.'

A stupid lie, thought Lionel, who could clearly see her work uniform underneath her overcoat.

The dog met them in the hall of Christopher's house. It was happy to have human company, but neither of them could be bothered with it. They could think of nothing but themselves and each other. They went upstairs to the bedroom and closed the door. The dog followed them and lay outside with its nose pressed into the gap under the door, waiting for its master to reappear. They lay together on the bed dressed in their winter clothes, the compacted snow from the soles of their shoes melting on to the duvet cover. They lay still for a long while, bulky in their overcoats and scarves and gloves, their faces pressed together. The light gradually faded.

Then Angela turned her head and said, 'Chris, I've put rather a lot of weight on.'

Christopher said, 'I know, I love you.'

82

He turned her head back towards him and found her mouth and covered it with his own. She took her glove off and slid her hand inside the bulk of clothing around his neck and pulled him towards her, crushing his mouth against hers. She felt his tongue and his teeth with her own tongue and teeth. They removed as much clothing as they could without losing touch, breaking away only for seconds to remove shoes and boots and underwear.

When they were naked they knelt on the bed and each looked at the unfamiliar middle-aged body of the other. Christopher lovingly stroked the rolls of fat that Angela hated, and she touched the grey hair on his chest that reminded Christopher of his own grandfather whenever he caught sight of his naked self in the mirror. They kissed the fat and the skin tags and the moles and callouses and broken veins, and the wrinkles and bags that middle age had visited upon them, and each thought the other beautiful. Christopher could still feel the skeleton of her, and Angela recognised the young Christopher and began to love him now in middle age. 'We're together again,' he said, before he gathered her heavy breasts together and brought them towards his mouth.

Nineteen

Gregory rang Heavenly Travel in the late afternoon and asked to speak to Angela, but she wasn't at work. She was sitting on the end of the bed in the dark. She was holding hands with Christopher and looking out of the window on to the new white snow world. They were both naked. Christopher's semen was drying between her legs. Angela was talking about Gregory.

'I'm not going to say I didn't love him Chris, I did love him, but it was nothing like this.' Christopher squeezed her hand, but didn't look at her. She had asked him not to. She had also asked him not to talk about their dead baby.

'But I can't leave him.'

'You can't go home to him *now*,' said Christopher. 'Ring him up and tell him you're going to come and live with me, in this house.'

'I can't do that!' She almost laughed.

'We love each other don't we?' Christopher was puzzled now. What was stopping her from leaving a man she didn't love, and going to live with a man she did love?

'Yes, we love each other,' she answered, 'But I can't just walk out on seventeen years of marriage, not just like that, can I?'

Christopher didn't see the problem. He didn't know Gregory and he didn't want to. He wondered if he ought to tell Angela about this premonition he had of his own death; there might not be time to worry about Gregory's feelings. He turned his attention back to her. She was talking about mortgage payments and joint savings accounts, and a shared pension plan and a holiday that she and Gregory had planned in a hotel for January in Barbados. He saw that, apart from himself, his body, he had almost nothing else to offer her.

Angela knew that she was gabbling, but she couldn't stop herself from talking about money and her financial responsibilities, which she saw as an invisible web, entangling her and preventing her escape. In her mind's eye she travelled through the rooms of her house, noting their comfort and warmth, feeling the soft carpets under her feet, fingering the thick texture of the heavy curtains, the dark solidity of the furniture. She'd worked on the garden until there was a green lushness there that delighted her every summer. How could she leave her grape-vine, or the sweet-smelling jasmine that framed the kitchen window?

She saw a policeman at the door breaking the news. She saw herself weeping over Gregory's grave. She saw herself and Christopher in the garden, sitting at the iron table on the terrace, drinking wine in the fading light.

'I'll come to you when he dies,' she said.

'I hope he dies soon, then,' said Christopher. And he let go of her hand, and began to get dressed. It was time to walk the dog.

Twenty

Crackle and Tamara didn't understand the words the tall posh doctor used when he told them what was wrong with Storme. But after he'd finished talking, when he said to them both, 'Do you understand?' they said, 'Yes.'

'Is there anything you'd like to ask me?' he said.

They looked at each other and then looked at him and said, 'No.'

'Perhaps you'd like to go and have a cup of tea?' He wanted them out of the way. He couldn't bear the stench of them in the small hot room. He was disgusted by their stupidity. He knew, almost for certain, that the child's injuries were non-accidental. He had already informed the police. 'There's a cafeteria downstairs. She should be out of theatre by half-past seven.'

'Two hours,' said Tamara.

There was a big clock with severe black hands on the wall of the Parents' Room.

Congratulations, you can tell the bloody time, thought Mr Parker-Wright who was the father of Julian, Felix, Harriet and Jessica. All of whom, at that very moment, were at music practice in the dining room of the Georgian house his wife kept so beautifully. He would miss their bedtime again. He went to the door and held it open for Crackle and Tamara. Obediently they got up off the hard sofa which doubled as a bed at night, and walked out into the corridor. They passed the room where Storme was being prepared for exploratory surgery and were steered to the lift by Mr Parker-Wright.

'So if we need you, we'll find you . . . ?'

'We'll be downstairs,' said Crackle.

He couldn't wait to get outside. The heat was killing him. He was sweating under his leather, and he was desperate for a fag. When the lift door closed he battered the large 'No Smoking' sign with his fist.

'Fucking stupid!' he said. 'Just when you *need* a fag, when your kid's filled up with *tubes*, you can't have one.'

Tamara couldn't get the picture out of her mind. The one where

86

Storme was lying on a high cot, wearing no clothes, with a thick tube that looked like a vacuum-cleaner hose in her mouth, and other see-through tubes in her nose and wrists. The nappy-rash sores looked scarlet next to the pure white sheet on which she had been laid. The brightness of the overhead light illuminated the accumulated grime on her body. And she could see now that, apart from the big green bruise, there were other bruises; smaller and in the pastel colour range. Tamara had watched Mr Parker-Wright counting these bruises. He handled Storme's body as gently as a man taking fragile eggs from a nest. They wouldn't allow Tamara inside the room because of the germs, but they allowed her to look through a window in the door.

Occasionally the staff nurse and the other nurses would straighten up from their work on Storme, and look at her. Tamara wished that they would smile, but their faces were set hard, which wasn't fair because she was the mother of a baby who needed an emergency operation. Crackle couldn't bring himself to look through the window, he was too sensitive.

Every pale, wooden table in the cafeteria displayed a small Perspex sign which said, 'This is a non-smoking table.'

Crackle said, 'Fuck it, I'm going over the road.'

Tamara followed behind as Crackle plunged angrily into the lab-yrinth of corridors, looking for an exit. She knew the way out, but she dared not tell him, fearing the explosion of rage that she knew was coming. Mr Parker-Wright had spoken to him with the utmost cour-tesy, but had managed at the same time to convey the message that he thought Crackle was a total moron.

Tamara knew that Crackle was clever, he could read and write, and he knew a lot of things about the world. Rivers and South Africa, and music and Dennis Wheatley, the man who wrote the books Crackle kept by the bed. When they eventually got outside Crackle threw her a cigarette, which she failed to catch. It dropped on to the snow and he called her a 'stupid cunt' and hit her on the side of her head. But the blow didn't hurt her much and it wasn't on her face, so there wouldn't be a bruise. She dried her tears when they got to Veronica's Café.

'I love you *so* much,' she said to him, just before he pushed open the door.

Twenty-One

Mr Parker-Wright was rather pleased that it was his turn to choose the music. He didn't fancy operating on the poor little tot to anything jolly. He chose Bach: the suites for unaccompanied cello. The acoustics were superb in the operating theatre. It was all those hard surfaces. He'd had a good sound system installed at his own expense. It made the work, much of it routine, tolerable. The bureaucrats who now ran the hospital didn't like it. He'd had a memo saying it was 'setting a precedent'. He'd laughed and pinned it next to his year planner where a formidable number of working days were marked with red stars.

He knew that he was revered and even loved by both his staff and his patients. One complete wall of his office was covered in thank-you notes and children's drawings. It was well known that he had a sweet tooth. A drawer in the office filing cabinet was full of boxes of liquorice allsorts, his particular favourites.

As the sonorous notes of the cello reverberated around the theatre, he took a scalpel and opened up Storme's abdomen. 'Spleen's ruptured,' he said to his team. 'I'll take that nasty old thing out for you, my darling,' he said to Storme. 'You won't miss it.'

As he worked he hummed along with the cello. He knew every note. When the tape stopped there was silence, apart from the sound of the machines that were keeping Storme alive. There was none of the repartee that usually enlivened Mr Parker-Wright's operating sessions. He opened her skull and saw that there was fresh bleeding and clots on her brain. 'See,' he said savagely to Storme. 'That's what you do when you fall out of your cot.' Then he controlled himself and said quietly, 'They shouldn't be allowed to breed.'

His surgical registrar said, smilingly, 'And I'd always thought you were so liberal and humane, Jack.'

Mr Parker-Wright smiled back and said, 'Oh, but I am, I am, except on the question of eugenics. I'm with Hitler on that one.'

Afterwards, when Storme had been taken to the recovery room, and Mr Parker-Wright had gone to phone his wife, opinion was divided between those of his team who believed the eugenics remark and those who thought he'd been making one of his infamous black jokes.

Tamara wanted to return to the hospital as soon as she'd finished her coffee, but Crackle didn't see the point of hanging around in there.

'There's nothing we can *do*, is there?' he said.

'No, I know, but I just want to *be* there, Crack,' she said. She scraped flakes of black varnish from her fingernails using the long thumbnail of her right hand. Crackle watched her irritably. She looked a right *dog* tonight, he thought. Her spots were showing through that white shit she put on her face. And she'd got too thin; she was a bag of bones, apart from her belly.

From where he was sitting in the café he could see the prison where Bilko, his best friend in all the world was. And if he turned his head, he could see the hospital where his little daughter was having an operation. His eyes filled with tears. Nothing ever went right for him, not for long.

'Shall I phone my dad and tell him?' Tamara had already got a twenty-pence piece in her hand.

'No.'

'I ought to tell him. He worships her.'

'He'll be pissed by now. I don't want him at the hospital pissed.'

Tamara put the twenty-pence piece back in her pocket.

Crackle stared down into his coffee cup and mentally catalogued his problems.

He owed £750 to Neville's Motors for a car which he'd crashed after three days because the brakes failed him on a tight bend. Then there was the poll tax and the council tax. Fuck knows how much that was. Then there was Kerry – a girl in Nottingham who reckoned he was the father of the kid she was expecting. But it couldn't be him because he'd only shagged her twice! He'd heard his brother was looking for him and threatening to kick his head in over the money he'd borrowed. Then he was up in court on December 22nd for driving whilst disqualified, no tax, no insurance, which everybody did. So why was he the only one stopped by the police? He didn't even have the poxy car no more. There were other things: he'd missed two appointments with his probation officer and the social were on his back. They'd found out he was living with Tamara. He'd stopped opening their letters. They were in a pile on top of the telly with other important documents like

Storme's birth certificate and the lottery tickets. Then there was the crack.

He was sick of his life.

Crackle wondered what Bilko was doing right now. Was he in his cell or was he having a laugh with some of his mates on the wing? Crackle was almost aggrieved that he'd never been sent to prison. It was humiliating to be given a community service order. Digging the garden at a hostel for loonies wasn't a proper punishment. He wanted a man's punishment. He'd done some bad things in his time. For two weeks he'd done the water scam, telling old people that he'd got to turn the water off in their bathroom, and nicking stuff out their bedrooms. They always kept their valuable stuff and their money in their bedside drawers. The stupid fuckers deserved to have it took off 'em.

He'd only done it for two weeks because on the Friday of the second week he'd been caught by an old woman. He'd *told* her to turn both the taps on in the kitchen and wait until he called her to turn them off, but she'd grassed him up and called the police. He'd heard her shouting down the phone; she was deaf. She'd told him on the doorstep he'd have to speak up. He hadn't meant to knock into her in the hallway; she got in the way. It made him feel bad when he saw her picture in the paper. Her name was Mrs Iris Knott and she was eighty-five. Crackle couldn't work out how her face had got in such a mess; she must have fell on something. He would never hit an old lady. He wasn't an animal like it said in the paper. Further down the page, after Crackle's description, Mrs Knott had appealed to the thief for the return of her engagement ring. She'd worn it for sixty-seven years and had only taken it off because she had lost weight, and she was afraid that it would slip off her finger. Crackle had seriously thought about giving the ring back to her, but how would he get it to her? He couldn't remember the number of the road she lived on, and anyway it was worth nothing, he'd only got fifteen quid for it. She shouldn't have put it in the bedside-table drawer. Old people should be warned. The government should do it, thought Crackle.

Tamara scraped her chair back and stood up. 'Two hours is gone,' she said.

'Sit *down*,' said Crackle.

'*Please*, Crack,' said Tamara. But she sat down. She knew Crackle liked to make the first move in anything. He warned her about it when they first got together. The first move and the last word.

While she waited for him she looked out of the window at the hospital. She could just about see it through the falling snow.

Waiting for them in the corridor at the hospital, next to the room where Storme lay in a tangle of tubes and wires, was a social worker, Kevin McDuff, and a policewoman, PC Billings. Mr Parker-Wright brought everybody into his office and informed Crackle and Tamara that it was his clinical opinion that Storme's injuries were non-accidental.

'Are you sayin' we done it?'

Crackle was outraged.

'I'm saying *somebody* did it. Somebody bigger and stronger than a fourteen-month-old child. There are two old fractures. Do you want to see the X-rays?' He didn't wait for an answer; he pulled an X-ray from a buff-coloured folder and slapped it up against a brightly lit box on the wall.

'She would have sustained this one', he pointed to one of Storme's X-rayed ribs, 'when she was about four months old, and this one', he indicated the bone in her upper arm, 'about three months later. She would have been in considerable pain. She must have cried . . .' He looked from Crackle to Tamara and waited.

'She did used to cry a lot,' said Tamara. 'I used to give her Calpol.'

'The mother's friend,' said Mr Parker-Wright ironically. Kevin McDuff nodded in recognition. 'Calpol is a liquid sedative,' he explained to PC Billings, whom he assumed, from the set of her jaw, to be childless. 'We quite often find our mothers slipping it to their little ones, in here.'

But she said, 'I know all about Calpol. I used it myself when mine were teething.'

Crackle said, 'So, what's happening then?'

Mr Parker-Wright said, 'As Storme's consultant I am formally advising Mr McDuff here and PC Billings that you and your partner are not to be allowed any kind of access to Storme whilst she is in my care in this hospital.'

Crackle shouted, 'You can't do that!'

Mr Parker-Wright continued, 'She is a very poorly little girl and right now, she *is* actually fighting for her life.'

'I love the ground that kid walks on,' said Crackle. He had tears in his eyes again. Now the bastards were preventing him from seeing his kid.

Tamara said, 'I've never hit her hard, just a little smack when she's been naughty; playing with the electric . . .' Her voice trailed away into teary incomprehensibility.

PC Billings said, 'Who did it to her, Tamara? If it wasn't you, who was it?'

Tamara put her head down on Mr Parker-Wright's desk and closed her eyes and covered her ears. The bad thing that she always knew would come one day had arrived.

Twenty-Two

When Angela got home Gregory was there, waiting for her. 'What's all this about a family crisis?' he asked her.

Angela had prepared a story on the way home. 'I couldn't stand it at work today,' she said. 'I'm under stress, Gregory.' Stress was a word that Gregory responded to. He claimed to suffer from it himself whenever he did his VAT returns. Only recently he had bought an anti-stress tape, a recording of a family of whales calling to each other, which he played in the car as an antidote to road-rage.

'So where have you been all day?' he said, as he filled the kettle.

'Just walking about,' she lied, taking off her coat and hanging it on the back of the pantry door.

'Are you going in tomorrow?' he said.

'Oh yes,' she said, eager to finish this conversation. 'I feel so much better now. Will pasta be all right for dinner?'

Gregory watched her carefully as she chopped and peeled and stirred. There was something different about her, but he couldn't quite define it. It was something to do with how she held her body. It was almost as if she'd forgotten that she was fat. She set the table carefully and opened a bottle of his favourite Valpolicella. There was warm bread and a green salad with an olive-oil dressing, and a rich sauce, and the pasta was soft, just how he liked it. And to follow there was Neapolitan ice cream with a crunchy triangular wafer which she knew he loved.

As she watched him eat, she thought there was something different about his face. He looked peculiar, unfinished. He lifted his linen napkin to his lips and dabbed it. When he put it back on to his lap, she realised.

'You've shaved your moustache off!' she said.

Gregory used a corner of the tablecloth to polish the convex back of the stainless-steel spaghetti server. When it was shining to his satisfaction, he gazed at his distorted reflection. He was pleased with what he saw.

'I'm doing something about my hair tomorrow,' he said. 'I'm going to be a new man,' he said with no discernible sign of humour. At least none that Angela could see.

Twenty-Three

Storme would never remember it except as a feeling. Very bright light would remind her of something of the agony. She couldn't cry out and expel any of the pain because there was something in her throat. She wanted to pull it out, but she couldn't move her arms. A woman's voice called her name. Storme opened her eyes and the light was like the sun. The voice murmured to her and she felt herself being touched and wanted to cry out again and pull away. Pictures came inside her head. She saw granddad's dog, Brandy, the door to the living room where the paint had bubbled, the pavement outside a shop, her mother's face and the red boots, and her father's face, and the window near her cot at home, and the bright colours of the television screen she sat in front of for most of the day and night. She heard echoing metal noises and softer shushing sounds. Helped by the maximum amount of pain-killers allowed to a child of her age and weight, she sank into a deeper unconsciousness. Imperceptibly her body started to recover from the iniquitous acts that had been done to it and began to heal.

Twenty-Four

The next morning Angela left the house an hour earlier than usual, telling Gregory that because of her absence yesterday, she would need to catch up. It isn't money that makes the world go round, it's lies, she thought, as she backed her car out of the driveway. She drove straight to Christopher's house. He was there waiting for her, on the doorstep, with the dog. He had changed the sheets and placed a lamp which cast a pink glow next to the bed.

This time when they made love, their old words came back to them. They had never written these words down because until the big break they had never been apart. And anyway, they were words to be sighed and breathed in an incoherent expression of love and desire. When they were still again, they stared into each other's eyes and smiled, then laughed out loud at the joy of being together again.

'If I could give you *anything*, anything in the world, what would it be Angie?' he said.

'Another hour in this bed,' she said, glancing at her watch, which said 8.30 a.m.

'No, what would it be?' said Christopher, insistently.

'It would be a baby,' she lied.

'Is that possible, Angela?' he said. She bent down to kiss his mouth. It tasted of her own salty juices.

'No, it's not possible, Chris. I've been sterilised,' she said. She lifted a roll of fat and showed him a two-inch scar just above her pubic hair.

'When did that happen?' His voice was flat with disappointment.

'It didn't just *happen*,' she said. 'That makes me sound as though it was something that was *done* to me against my will. *I* phoned the Elms. *I* booked in. *I* paid the money. *I* willingly had the operation. I came out of there three days later, sterile. It was what I wanted.' She got out of bed and reached for her underwear.

'Please don't look at me,' she said. He turned his head away and looked at the wall opposite the window. He listened to her breathy exertions as she dressed; he heard the snap of elastic and the rustle of nylon on nylon.

'How soon after were you sterilised?' he said.

'Do you mean how soon after I left you?'

'Yes.'

'I went straight there, from the house.'

He sat up in bed. 'You arranged it while we were still living together?'

'Yes. And don't say you weren't told, Chris, because I *told* you over and over again that I would never have another baby.' She was fully dressed now, in the uniform that didn't suit her. 'But you didn't *listen* to me because *you* wanted one.'

'I thought you were saying it because of what happened to you. I thought, as time went on . . .'

'As time went on', she shouted, 'you developed an *obsession* about having another baby. It was all you talked about.'

He got out of bed, naked and furious.

'Is it unnatural to want a baby?'

'Yes, it is, it is, if your partner doesn't want one. If your partner feels that all she is, is a potential carrier for *your* baby.'

'You were jealous,' he said. 'Of a baby that wasn't even born.'

'Yes, I was,' she shouted. 'It was my love rival. It was as if you were planning to fall in love with another woman and bring her to live in our house, and share our bed.' Tears came into her eyes. 'I mustn't cry,' she said. 'I look terrible when I cry. My eyes are swollen for days.'

He put his hands on her shoulders while she wiped her eyes and blew her nose on a tissue she took from her handbag.

'There are different kinds of love, Angie,' he said.

'So you tell me,' she said. 'But it's too late now, isn't it?'

Twenty-Five

When they eventually left the hospital Tamara was crying. She'd tried to stop. She knew it got on Crackle's nerves. She could see by the way his cheekbones moved that he was upset himself, but his eyes were dry. She'd tried to take his hand, but he'd slapped her off. His silence terrified her. They went into a telephone box and she rang for a taxi, but snow had started falling again, and the man on the end of the phone said that they would have to wait forty minutes. When she'd told Crackle he had said, 'Fuck that,' stomped out of the telephone box and headed towards the city centre. She hadn't dared to follow him, but had watched his hunched figure until he'd turned the corner at the top of the street.

Earlier on in the café she'd given him all the money she had. She waited, shivering, inside the box until the taxi came over an hour later. She gave the driver an address which wasn't hers, but which was round the corner from where she lived. As they drew near to the false destination, she stealthily opened the door of the car and leapt out, before it had come to a complete standstill. As she darted across the road and ran up an alley between two rows of houses, she heard the driver's shout of rage as he watched his fare disappear into the night.

She opened the back garden gate of a house and crouched down in the darkness by the shed wall. She listened to the sound of the taxi as it drove around the block, then hearing the engine accelerate and die away, she crept out of the garden and walked the long way round to the flat. The phone started ringing as she turned the key to the front door. She ran into the living room and snatched it up, expecting it to be somebody from the hospital telling her that Storme was dead. But it was Crackle asking her to find her benefit book, and get a taxi and take it to Rita's crack house where he'd been refused credit. She could hear music in the background and raucous laughter.

'I can't, I feel poorly,' she said, and it was true. She felt as though her body was full of poison. All she wanted to do was to lie down and rest. He was incredulous. He screamed at her, causing his voice to rise in pitch like that of a woman.

'Bring it *now*. I need it! Bring it now!'

'I've got to stay here, in case the hospital ring,' she pleaded.

'I'll kill you,' he screamed. 'I'll fucking mark your face.'

She put the phone down on him, then fetched the red coat, pulled it around her and lay down on the sofa. She dare not go to bed, and it was true that she couldn't bear to leave the phone. Eventually sleep overcame her.

She heard him stumble in. It was still dark. She braced herself for a beating, hiding her face with her hands and pulling her legs up so that her knees were pressed against her breasts. But he passed down the hallway and went into the bedroom. She heard him undressing and getting into bed. She waited, alive to every sound, until she heard the snores that told her that he was asleep. Only then did she uncoil her body and allow herself to drift off again into a troubled dream world.

In the morning Tamara got up from the sofa and went to the phone to find that it had now been disconnected, as British Telecom had threatened. Pausing only to grab her make-up bag from the bathroom, she left the flat before Crackle woke up and started on her.

She hurried as fast as she could through the snow, slithering in the only dry footwear she'd got, the black cowboy boots with the worn-down heels. Her dad lived less than a mile away on the same estate, but the snow turned the journey into an exhausting epic. Tamara felt like a fugitive, she half-expected Crackle's face to appear in the sky, and his voice to order her back.

Tamara's father, Ken, checked to see who it was at his front door at 8.30 a.m. in the morning, by peering down from the bedroom window upstairs. It was many years since he'd been able to open the door without hesitation. There was always some bugger at the door asking for money. He'd tried to keep out of debt, but as soon as he got clear something else happened to knock him back – like finding the money for Cath's headstone.

He didn't look pleased to see Tamara. She always brought trouble with her. If it was money she wanted, he'd give her a fiver and no more.

Ken said, 'What's up now?' They were a family who didn't bother with greetings or goodbyes.

'Storme's in the hospital.' Tamara dreaded the inevitable next question.

'What's up with her?'

Brandy, the fat Labrador sniffed at Tamara's crotch. She pushed him away.

'She fell out of her cot. She's got a fractured skull and they've took her spleen out.'

Ken fumbled in the pocket of his burgundy towelling dressing gown for his cigarettes and lighter, and went into the kitchen and picked up the mug of tea he'd been drinking when Tamara had knocked at the door. The *Daily Mirror* was propped against the sugar bowl, it was open at a picture spread of the Spice Girls. The kitchen was as clean and neat as it had always been when her mother had been alive. He sat down heavily on a mock pine chair and raked back his thinning brown hair with his fingers. Tamara looked at him and wondered when it was he had got so old.

'Our phone's been cut off. Can I ring and ask how she is?'

Ken gestured wearily towards the wall phone in the kitchen. It was one bleddy thing after another, he thought. When would it end? His body felt heavy and he was reluctant to get off the chair and go upstairs and get dressed.

'Poor little bugger,' he said. 'I'll get myself sorted and we'll go and see her.'

Tamara was speaking to directory enquiries, asking for the number of the hospital. 'Tamara!' shouted Ken. 'Don't phone bleddy enquiries at over a quid a shot. It's up there, on the wall!'

A year ago when Cath was alive, he had neatly written out a list of the telephone numbers they used the most and pinned it to the cork noticeboard next to the telephone. Since then the words 'Cath's work' had had three lines drawn through them. He had used the edge of a cigarette packet as a ruler to ensure that the lines were absolutely straight. Cath should be *here*, he thought. She was needed. She always knew what to do. Why hadn't God taken that pile of shit, Crackle, instead? Ken had banned Crackle from the house since that hot day when he had taken his t-shirt off in the back garden and Ken had seen that the scumbag had paid good money to have 'Satan' tattooed in inch-high letters across his shoulders.

Ken and Cath were Christians and had braved the derision of their family and friends and fellow council tenants and had gone to morning service on Sundays at the concrete Anglican church that looked like a fire station. The congregation struggled to reach double figures. Ken had stopped going to church after Cath's funeral. He hadn't wanted to be told by the deaconess who conducted the service that Cath had been born and had died in sin. If it was true, then what was the point of living? He prayed on his own now. After he'd turned the television off at night.

Tamara put the phone down and said, 'They say she's still very poorly.'

They had to push the Volkswagen Golf to get it started. A man sweeping snow from his path came to help them. Love thy neighbour, thought Ken. He was glad he had resisted having a tot of whisky in his tea. God must have known he'd need to drive the car and have a clear head.

When they'd parked the car and were walking across the gritted hospital carpark, Ken pressed Tamara for more details about the accident. He knew from the familiar way that her index finger flew to her mouth that she was lying to him.

When he spoke to Mr Parker-Wright an hour later, he knew for certain who had harmed his little granddaughter. He felt as if his head would explode with anger. He was not a violent man, but there and then he vowed to kill Crackle. He would do it himself. You couldn't trust God to mete out the proper punishment to Satan's disciples. Not nowadays. God had gone soft on crime.

Twenty-Six

Crackle woke up and found himself alone in the cold bedroom. No Tamara next to him and no Storme in her cot. Then he remembered.

He felt like crying but he didn't know how to get the tears out any more. They were locked inside him: these tear-shaped pieces of rock. His whole body was full of them; sometimes he wondered how he managed to walk around carrying such a heavy weight. If he was cut open, like Storme was last night, they wouldn't find no blood in his veins, just these little shining tear-shaped rocks.

After lighting a cigarette, he got out of bed and wrapped himself in a blanket. He shouted, 'Tamara', but she didn't shout back. Something must have happened. She never went out or did anything without telling him first. He went to the window and drew the curtain aside. The estate was strangely becalmed by the snow. As he watched, a car drove slowly along the slip road and parked in front of the flats. PC Billings and Kevin McDuff got out and looked up at the flats. Had Tamara blabbed to the police and done a runner? Crackle let go of the curtain and bent over the pile of black clothes he'd thrown on to the floor beside the bed the night before. They were cold to the touch and he shivered as he put them on.

When he'd been a little boy he'd dressed in front of the gas fire in the living room on winter mornings. His real mother had made him eat a bowl of porridge before he'd gone to school. He remembered her running after him once because he'd forgotten his gloves. He'd been ashamed because he'd been with Bilko, who didn't believe in gloves.

He was fastening the death's head buckle on his belt when the knock came on the door. As he went to answer it he practised what he would say if they accused him of hurting Storme.

He opened the door and they stepped back slightly as the smell from the flat rushed out on to the stone cold landing.

'I need to do a home report,' said Kevin.

Crackle opened the door and ushered them inside. PC Billings covered her nose and mouth with a gloved hand. The air in the flat felt thick, as though it were saturated with bodily secretions.

'I tried ringing,' said Kevin. 'Did you know your phone's been cut off?'

'Bastards,' said Crackle. It was Tamara's fault. She was always ringing them 0891 numbers to find out what her stars had lined up for her. She was a Libra.

Kevin knew the layout of the flats and he led the way into the bedroom. All three of them looked down into the cot. The smell of urine was already overpowering, but became worse when PC Billings pulled aside the damp blankets to reveal the soaked mattress, which was stained with faeces and dried-on blood.

'And this is where she slept?' asked PC Billings.

'Yeah, but she kept climbing out of it,' said Crackle.

'I'm not surprised,' said the PC. 'It's not exactly Mothercare in there, is it?'

She circumnavigated the chaotic piles of things on the floor and walked out of the bedroom and looked at the other rooms. The hopeless squalor of the place disorientated her. She didn't know where to begin to describe it in her notebook. And it was *so cold*. Her breath fanned out in front of her. She sorted through the documents on top of the television and amongst the unopened DSS letters and lottery tickets and British Telecom threats, she found Storme's birth certificate, a prison visiting order, and what seemed to be a poem written in crabbed handwriting on the back of a large white envelope. Before she could read the poem Crackle came into the room with Kevin and she put the envelope back on the pile. Crackle said, 'Do you know how she is this morning?'

Kevin said, 'I rang the hospital before I came out. She's comfortable.'

'Comfortable,' repeated Crackle. 'That's good.'

'Comfortable means nothing,' said PC Billings. 'They said it about a bloke I knew with sixty-degree burns and a broken pelvis. Poor sod only lived three days.'

She wouldn't give Crackle any comfort. If she couldn't get him for physically abusing his kid, she'd get him for neglect, and if she had to drag that disgusting mattress into court as evidence, she would.

Meanwhile, she would take Crackle back to the police station with her before he could start clearing the place up. She wanted the police photographer to capture its insane chaos.

Twenty-Seven

Angela thought that Veronica's Café would be a safe place for her to meet Christopher at lunchtime. Gregory never went near the east end of the city. She arrived there first and was glad because it gave her time to do her hair and make-up in the squalid lavatory next to the kitchen. Christopher was there, sitting at a table furthest from the window, when she came out. The dog was already asleep at his feet. He looked up and saw her and raised his arm as though she was not five steps away, but was instead approaching him from the end of a long road. They had to touch each other. He helped her to take her coat off but, instead of hanging it up on a peg on the wall near by, he laid it across the table and they held hands beneath it for a while before Angela removed it and hung it over the back of her chair. She looked around. The café didn't look so bad today. Nothing had changed physically: but Angela saw it now with the eyes of a duplicitous woman. The grimy surfaces and the bad food spoke to her now of human fallibility.

Christopher gazed at her lovely face, and pushed back a strand of hair that had attached itself to the corner of her mouth. It was another excuse to touch her. He wanted her again. He wanted her back in his bed. He told her this.

'I want you as well,' she said. She remembered his morning face as his semen pumped inside her. He had opened his eyes and told her to open hers, and they had held their gaze until he was empty, and she was full of him.

She was wearing a pink silk scarf at her neck. He touched it and said, 'I didn't notice that scarf this morning. It's lovely.'

'Thank you,' she said. 'I bought it on the way here. It's a Hermès copy.'

'I'll buy you a real Hermès scarf one day,' he said. 'We'll go to Paris, on the Eurostar.'

He asked what she wanted to eat, but she shook her head and said, 'I can't eat, Chris; I've had nothing since yesterday morning.'

It was true. She felt bloated with love. There was no room for food.

She watched him when he went to the counter to order his own food. Whilst he waited for the café woman with the lank hair to remove a wire basket full of pale chips from the deep fat frier, he turned to look at Angela and smiled and mimed drinking a cup of tea. She nodded and he turned around and gave the woman his order. As he started back to the table he saw Tamara, Storme's mother, come into the café with her arm around a man of his own age. The man was dabbing at his eyes with a tissue. He heard Tamara's loud whisper, 'Don't, Dad' and the man's reply, 'I can't help it, sorry.'

Tamara steered her father to the table next to Angela and Christopher, and seated him gently. He turned his back away from them and blew his nose loudly. It wasn't until Christopher said hello to her that Tamara recognised him as the man who'd bought Storme the red boots and the snowsuit. He was sitting with a fat woman with black shiny hair and red lipstick. Tamara said hello back to him and turned to her dad, who was folding the tissue into a neat square before putting it into one of his trouser pockets. She was glad her dad had stopped crying. It was a terrible thing to see and hear. It made her feel as if blackness was going to cover the earth.

'Shall I get you a cup of tea?'

Ken didn't trust himself to speak. He'd need a couple of minutes. He shook his head. What he wanted, needed, was the compassionate bite of alcohol at the back of his throat. He'd have a pint of mild first, and follow it with a treble Johnnie Walker. He needed to forget what he had seen at the hospital, and the shame he had felt when his daughter had been ordered away from Storme's bedside by Mr Parker-Wright.

'Will you come to the police station with me, Dad?'

Ken nodded. He'd have to try and walk that dividing line between drunkenness and apparent sobriety. It was going to be difficult: Tamara's appointment with PC Billings was at four o'clock which left him three hours' drinking time. He could throw a lot down his neck in three hours. He'd have to take it steady: pace himself. He lit two cigarettes and passed one to Tamara.

'You'd better go home and do yourself up,' he said. 'You look bleddy awful.'

He was ashamed to be sitting with her, looking like she did.

'I can't go home,' said Tamara. 'And anyway I've got nothing else to put on.' Cath had kept her looking like a little princess. They called her their pink princess, because it was the only colour she would wear. Now she only wore black.

There were photograph albums in the unit in his living room that showed they'd brought her up properly. There was page after page of Tamara looking clean and healthy and happy, smiling delightedly into the camera. Her pink dresses always ironed, her long blonde hair plaited or bunched, or flowing over her shoulders. Her white socks turned at the ankle. He couldn't reconcile that pretty little girl with the pasty-faced young woman who sat opposite him now. He would never understand why she'd dyed her beautiful hair black and shaved most of it off. He watched her picking at the loose threads in her black sweater, then he took his wallet out and pulled two twenty-pound notes from the compartment inside. He passed them to Tamara and said, 'Here, go and buy something. I'm not going to the police station with you looking like that.'

From inside another plastic compartment of the wallet Cath's photograph stared up at him. A first-class stamp obscured part of her face. Ken pushed the stamp aside and looked at Cath. She'd not been a pretty woman, but she'd been a lovely wife. There was no point in looking for a replacement. It was just a matter of getting through the rest of his days without her.

Christopher had seen Ken pass the money to Tamara and was pleased. He would have been a generous father himself, he thought; a soft touch.

'How's your little girl?' he asked Tamara. He couldn't bring himself to say Storme's ridiculous name. She didn't answer, but instead looked at her father as though asking for permission before replying. Christopher noticed her discomfiture and said, awkwardly, 'Does she still like her red boots?'

Tamara said, 'She's in the hospital,' and indicated the building over the road where the lighted windows of the wards could be seen vividly through the dark light caused by the cambered snow clouds above. 'She fell out of her cot.'

Angela saw the shock on Christopher's face and turned around to take a proper look at this girl who was apparently a mother, but had the voice of a child. When Tamara eventually disclosed the extent of Storme's injuries Christopher half rose to his feet. His body needed to move. Angela put a restraining hand on his arm and he sat down at once. He remembered Storme walking proudly in her new boots. Angela was bewildered by this girl's passionless account of the accident to her baby.

'She was *told* not to do it. I told her, and her dad told her, but she kept doing it, climbing out. Then she must have just – fell.'

Angela said, 'On to a bare floor?'

'No, there's a carpet,' said Ken.

Blood was thicker than water. What had their family business got to do with these strangers?

'And this fall fractured her skull and ruptured her spleen?' Christopher asked.

Tamara looked away.

'She must have landed funny,' said Ken.

He clasped his hands together. He was trembling for a drink.

The café woman shouted from the serving hatch that Christopher's ham salad and chips were ready. But it was Angela who got up to collect it. She wanted to do things for him. She made a second journey to collect their cups of tea and then a third to collect paper napkins and cutlery and salt and pepper. She arranged everything in front of him as though she were making preparations for a simple religious ceremony. She wanted him to know that she worshipped him.

She was pleased to see that the girl and her father were preparing to leave. She resented the interruption they had caused to the short time she and Christopher had together. As Tamara and Ken got up to leave, Christopher said, 'I'll be thinking about her.'

When they were outside on the icy pavement, Ken said, 'Who's he?'

Tamara said, 'Just a bloke,' and she took her father's arm. He looked unsteady on his feet.

Angela watched Christopher eating. She loved the neat way he cut his food up and forked it into his mouth. She bent down and stroked the sinuous back of the dog and it woke and pushed its muzzle into her hand. 'I love your dog,' she said.

'We'll go and see the baby when I've finished this,' he said, looking over at the hospital.

'I can't go,' she said. 'I've got to go back to work. And they won't let you see her will they? You're not family are you?'

'I just want to see her,' he said, stubbornly. 'Come with me, Angie.'

They were careful to keep a distance between them as they crossed the road together. Nobody seeing them would have known that they were lovers. When they drew near to the entrance of the hospital Angela looked at her watch and said, 'I'll be late for work if I don't go now.' He pleaded with her to accompany him. Helplessly she agreed. He tied the dog's lead to the icy iron railings surrounding a small frosty garden and they went inside.

At the main reception he gave the little information he knew about Storme and after a short wait they were told that Storme was on the seventh floor, in Paediatric Intensive Care. Angela was relieved. There was no possibility of visiting anyone there. If she started back now she wouldn't be late for work. But Christopher walked towards the lifts and pressed the button for the seventh floor.

'You can't!' she said.

'Please, Angie, come with me,' he said.

The lift was empty, and he took her in his arms as soon as the doors shut. When they opened again he said, 'Just look as if you know where you're going.'

There was nobody at the nurses' station at the entrance to the ward. Nobody came to answer the ringing telephone.

Christopher soon found Storme. He stood looking through the glass at her, and at the nurses who were threading a plastic tube inside her nose.

Angela looked for a moment, then turned her head away and went back to the lift to wait for him. Catherine came and stood at her side. As usual, she was immaculately groomed. Her school uniform looked brand new.

'I might be a doctor, Mum,' she said. 'I'll need three good science A levels and one in English. What do you think?' Her voice was melodious, like an angel's.

'You can do anything; you're the cleverest girl I know,' said Angela. Then she said, 'You didn't come to see me yesterday.'

Catherine laughed, 'You were busy, Mum, with Dad.'

Angela asked her, 'Are you pleased about me and Dad getting together again?'

Catherine kissed the top of her mother's head and said, 'Of course, it's great to have two parents.'

Angela said, 'You're a wonderful, perfect daughter.'

Angela and Christopher stood in the lift in silence for a while. Suddenly he took her hand and said, 'You've got to tell me about the day you killed our baby.'

Angela hit him hard across his face with the flat of her right hand.

The lift stopped on the third floor and a porter pushing an old man in a wheelchair, got in. The old man looked at Christopher and Angela and passed a hand over the grey stubble on his face.

'I need a shave,' he said apologetically.

Angela didn't wait for Christopher while he untied the dog from the railings but he soon caught up with her. He said, 'Call in at my house tonight Angie. Please.' Her face was closed in. She wouldn't look at him. He dropped back ten paces, and walked all the way behind her, only leaving her when he saw that she was safely inside Heavenly Holidays.

Twenty-Eight

Crackle lay on the hard bed in the police cell and did that trick with his mind that detached him from humiliating and painful circumstances. It was a knack he had. He'd had it since he was a little kid. It had come to him on a Maundy Thursday in school assembly. They were singing 'There is a green hill far away' and Crackle had suddenly known what it must have been like to be Jesus. To have nails hammered through his hands and feet, and to be left to hang from the cross until he was dead. Crackle had stopped singing, the breath had left his body and he couldn't feel his hands or his feet. He had sat down on the floor of the assembly hall, surrounded by the legs of the other children. He couldn't find the words to explain to the headmaster what had happened to him. So he had remained sitting down and had said nothing. It was during the headmaster's angry denunciation of him in front of the school that Satan had come to him.

Crackle distanced himself from the police cell and thought about the person he loved most in the world: Bilko. Bilko had always protected Crackle both from his enemies and from Crackle's own foolishness since they were at junior school together. Bilko had joined the class half-way through the autumn term, long after alliances had been formed and a pecking order established.

Thirty-five white ten-year-olds, boys and girls had listened to Mrs McLuskey, the class teacher's nervous preamble. 'We've got a new boy joining us today. His name is James Billington. I'll be bringing him into our classroom quite soon. Before I do that I'd like to ask you to be *especially* kind to him. Be tolerant. It's not easy joining a class half-way through a term. I wonder, is there anybody who'd like to be his special friend and show him around the school?'

Mrs McLuskey scanned the room. Nobody lifted an arm. She sighed and said again, '*Please* be kind to him.' Then she left the room to collect the mysterious James Billington, who for some reason needed their kindness.

An excited chatter broke out as soon as she'd closed the classroom door. There was speculation about the boy. Crackle, who was one of the class clowns, mimicked Mrs McLuskey's Glaswegian accent. 'Be kind to him, be tolerant.'

Crackle was not popular. His kitchen-scissors haircut and hand-me-down shoes betrayed his extreme poverty, and only a few children laughed.

When Mrs McLuskey returned she had the boy with her. His skin was black and his hair was braided in dozens of thin plaits. The boy, James Billington, was dressed in a scaled-down version of adult clothes. He looked straight ahead, seemingly engrossed by the contour lines of a map of South America, which hung on the back wall of the classroom. Mrs McLuskey said, 'This is James. Say hello to him, please.' The class droned, 'Hello James.'

When Crackle put his hand up and said, 'He can sit next to me, Miss,' giggles broke out and somebody shouted, 'Poofter.' When the boy sat down next to him Crackle could hear that James was breathing very fast, and he knew that the boy's induction into the class had been an ordeal for him.

At playtime James Billington leaned against a wall with Crackle and watched the white children mill around in the playground. He spoke for the first time.

'What they runnin' around for?' he said. 'They ain't *goin'* no place.'

'You're American!' said Crackle.

'No, Jamaican, but I've been living in New York City, with my dad.'

Crackle was impressed. He had heard of New York. It was where the Mafia lived.

'Why have you come to live here?'

'My dad sent me to live with my mum.'

Crackle looked beyond the playground to the Bevan, as the estate was called. He'd lived there all his life in one of those little cramped houses. 'Why, what did you do wrong?' said Crackle.

'I din't do *nothin'* wrong.' James plunged his hands deep into the pockets of his baggy jeans. 'My dad got married again.'

Crackle understood at once. He himself had been passed around like an unwanted parcel since his real mum had left home and he had somehow ended up living with his second stepfather and his step-father's new wife. He knew that neither of them wanted him: the whereabouts of his next move was a daily topic of conversation. Crackle wanted to live with his real mum again, but she had moved in with a man called Barry, who couldn't stand children. There was a rumour that this Barry had a white carpet in his living room.

For a few weeks Crackle guided his new friend, now called Bilko by everybody, around the estate; warning him about which streets to avoid, and which persons might give him grief. Then one day, after a fight with a rival school, when Bilko had saved him from a good kicking, the roles were reversed and it was Crackle who looked to Bilko to guide him through the many difficulties he encountered in his life.

It was Bilko who had later warned him not to touch crack cocaine. They were both twenty-four years old, and were in the kitchen of Bilko's luxuriously furnished council flat. It was a superior block which had a security guard on the door, and closed-circuit cameras in the well-kept public areas. Bilko was a fastidious man. He couldn't have lived in the shit holes that Crackle lived in.

They were in the kitchen. Crackle was watching Bilko iron a pile of Ralph Lauren shirts. The steamy smell reminded Crackle of his real mother. Crack had recently arrived in the city and Bilko had seen that there was big money to be made out of supplying it. But he was doing OK with his own specialist business – selling steroids to body-builders and athletes. He'd got most of the East Midlands covered. It was illegal, what he did, but he was hardly the evil drug pusher, was he? Some of his clients had won big competitions: there were six framed photographs grouped on one wall of his living room, showing his clients, victorious and smiling with their trophies and winners' sashes draped across their bulging chests.

He finished ironing another shirt, hung it on a hanger, buttoned it up carefully and gave it to Crackle, who took it through to the bedroom and hung it in one of the built-in wardrobes. A specialist firm had made them to Bilko's specification. Crackle stopped briefly to look at the photographs of Bilko's children displayed on top of a chest of drawers. They were happy-looking babies. When he went back into the kitchen Bilko was pushing the pointed end of the steam iron in between the buttons of another shirt. He could have had any number of women to do his ironing for him, but so far nobody came up to his exacting standards.

'Have you ever used crack, Bilko?' he asked.

'No, and I ain't going to neither. I've seen what it does to people.'

'What does it do then?' Crackle was intrigued.

'OK, they call it "licking the rock", OK? So the first time you lick the rock you get this fucking amazing high. So fucking amazing that there ain't words in the dictionaries to describe it, innit.'

'What, like coke?' Crackle had used cocaine when he could afford it. It had made him happy to be alive for once.

'No, no. It ain't *nothing* like coke. They call this stuff "the broken promise" because the second time you take it you're expecting the same amazing thing, innit? But the second time you don't get it as good, and you ain't *never* gonna get it as good, innit?' Bilko picked up the little jug and poured water into the funnel inside the iron. 'Because. The first time you took it, it destroyed some of the pleasure centres in your brain, so you ain't *never* gonna feel the same pleasure again. Not just with crack, but with sex and food and even fuckin' *music* man. So don't touch it eh, Crackle? Promise me, man.'

'Promise,' said Crackle. But within days, behind Bilko's back, he had gone to a crack house on a council estate on the eastern outskirts of the city, where a motherly woman called Rita had prepared his first crack hit.

Within seconds he experienced an ecstasy of sensation. He was blissfully aware of every vein in his body: they were coursing not with blood, but with sweet, sweet honey. His eyes saw the wondrous colours in Rita's room. He looked down at his hands and was transfixed by the beauty of his fingers. He knew *everything*. He was a superior being, the secrets and beauties of the universe were revealed to him. His body was an exquisite conductor of the magnificence of living.

Within twenty minutes he had shit himself. Diarrhoea spread out from the crotch of his jeans in a brown stain. Rita helped him to the bathroom and explained that it wasn't his fault. Crack was cocaine mixed with bicarbonate of soda and the bicarbonate of soda loosened the bowels. She fetched clean underpants and jeans from a stock she kept for the purpose and he cleaned himself up and changed into the clean clothes and joined the others in Rita's breakfast room, who were sitting in the dark, ascending to heaven or descending into hell.

Rita charged him nothing for his first time with crack. On his second visit she asked for thirty pounds. He gave it to her gladly, but the second time he took it it was just as Bilko had said it would be. It was a broken promise. Trouble was, his body kept on wanting it like it was the first time. Crackle was on a treadmill trying to catch up with that amazing sensation, but it was always in the distance, just out of reach.

When Bilko found out he wouldn't speak to him for a month. But then he relented and even paid off a few of his crack debts. When Bilko's other friends, the wearers of Hugo Boss suits and Timberland Shoes mocked Bilko for his philanthropy towards Crackle, Bilko shrugged his shoulders and said, 'Yeah, that Crackle's a sad bastard, but we go back a long way, innit.'

Twenty-Nine

The Man at Rest was owned and run by the licensee, Douglas Reginald Swainson. It said so above the door to the street. It was furnished and decorated entirely to Douglas's taste. There was no Mrs Swainson behind the bar to purse her lips and disapprove of the mixture of styles. In the Man at Rest a spindly cottage suite shared space with heavy oak tables and chairs he'd bought from a closed-down library. The walls and the ceiling were nicotine brown. Holiday postcards from regulars were crammed on the shelves behind the bottles and glasses. The rose-patterned carpet was stained with years of spillage. Douglas Swainson didn't like juke boxes or slot machines and he regarded pub food as an affectation.

Ken pushed the street door open and went into the one-roomed pub, and up to the bar. He put his foot on the tarnished brass rail and ordered a pint of mild and a whisky chaser from Douglas, who looked behind the beer pumps like a large pale ghost. Douglas disliked sunlight and kept it out of his pub. The curtains were permanently drawn. Ken nodded at the other regulars: Thin Bob, Fat Stan, Daft Arthur and Raj. Raj could get you anything: a joint of beef, a wedding suit, an engine for a car, anything, half price, no questions asked.

'What's up?' asked Douglas, observing that Ken didn't look himself. Ken soon had the regulars' full attention as he recounted his recent visit to the hospital and his suspicions about Crackle. His friends swore quietly to themselves as they listened to Ken's description of Storme's injuries. Douglas pushed another double whisky in front of Ken. 'On the house,' he said.

'I wish that fuckin' Crackle would walk in here right now,' said Thin Bob. 'I'd love to put my fist down his throat.'

'I want to *kill* him,' said Ken, throwing the whisky down the back of his throat.

'Anybody who hurts a baby like that *deserves* to die,' said Arthur. 'If one of mine was harmed . . .' the other men nodded their agreement. 'I'd gladly do bird,' said Stan, whose grandchildren irritated him on the rare occasions he was to be found at home.

Douglas said, 'Scum like that Crackle shouldn't be allowed to breed. In fact,' he said, 'if I was a dictator I'd make people pass a test before they could have a baby. They'd have to *pay* to get one; they'd need a licence.'

Ken was drunk, but not falling-over drunk when he left the Man at Rest and went out into the afternoon gloom. Raj caught up with him on the pavement, gripping him on the top of his arm. Ken swivelled around, ready to fight, only relaxing when he saw who it was. Raj bent his big-toothed brown face to Ken's ear and said, 'If you want that Crackle seeing to, I know somebody who'll do it for you.'

Ken staggered to the pub wall and leaned against it. The cold air was making his head spin. '*Seeing to?*' he said.

'Fifty quid for a good kicking,' said Raj. 'And two hundred and fifty quid to put him out, permanent.'

'Kill him, you mean?'

Raj was scandalised by the directness of Ken's query. 'Now *they* ain't the words I used, Ken,' said Raj, looking away and shaking his head.

'Sorry,' said Ken, aware now that he had breached some kind of criminal etiquette.

'Two hundred and fifty quid, though, that's cheap isn't it?'

Ken had thought that contract killing was something only the rich could afford.

'There's a lot of guns around,' said Raj. 'And a lot of crack heads desperate for money.'

'So I could put him away, *for ever* for a week's wages?' Ken was on the sick with his nerves, but he'd be going back to work soon. He thought hard for a moment, trying to imagine a world without Crackle. 'It sounds good,' he said to Raj. They walked around the corner to Raj's car repair workshop, and Raj got one of his mechanics to make Ken a black coffee in an attempt to sober him up before he went to the police station.

PC Billings put the phone down, then sat at the desk she shared with four colleagues and breathed in deeply, trying to calm herself. She'd rung home to check that Carole, the baby-sitter, had picked the kids up from school as arranged, but throughout their brief conversation she'd heard her boys, five-year-old Mark, and seven-year-old James, arguing. She heard Mark shout in his shrill voice, 'It wasn't *me*, tell him.' Then James's whine, 'Tell *him*.' She promised Carole she would be home soon after her shift finished at eight o'clock, and reminded her that there were fish fingers and oven chips in the deep freeze, and that when she gave Mark his bath she mustn't forget to put the anti-eczema oil in the water, else he'd be scratching all night. And another thing, would Carole make sure that James went to the loo before going to bed. He'd wet the bed again the night before.

She lifted her head and looked around the office. She was certain that none of her male colleagues had given a thought to the pre-bedtime rituals of their children. She got up and picked up the folder marked 'Storme Natas'. She'd thought it a peculiar surname, foreign sounding. Suddenly she realised that it was Satan spelled backwards. She was surprised the authorities had allowed them to use it. The whole case depressed her. She couldn't get the sight and smell of that cot mattress out of her mind. At ten past four the internal phone rang and the desk sergeant told her that there was a Mr Kenneth Dixon and a Mrs Tamara Natas at the front desk.

When they met at the police station Ken saw that Tamara had bought herself a loose black dress with a long skirt that swept the floor. It wasn't what he'd had in mind at all. He'd wanted her to buy something pretty, something motherly. I've wasted forty quid, he thought. A black leather thong with a pewter beast's head pendant hung between the swell of her breasts.

'Take that bleddy thing off,' he ordered, offended by the beast's green-eyed look of evil. Tamara did as she was told, slipping it off and stuffing it into the side pocket of the dress. She didn't want to upset her dad. He was already drunk.

She looked up each time one of the three doors leading into the front office opened. She knew that Crackle was somewhere in the police station, and she was desperate to see him, and tell him that she was sorry for running away from him. She looked at Ken, whose eyelids were drooping. He stank of drink. She slid along the plastic-covered bench and distanced herself from him. Without her physical support his head dropped back and he fell asleep with his mouth open, displaying the wire bridgework on his teeth. Tamara had known he would let her down. She took the pendant from out of her pocket and hung it around her neck again. When PC Billings came to fetch her they had both tried to wake her dad, but he had been unable to get to his feet without falling, so they had left him sitting on the bench with his head in his hands.

It was eight o'clock in the evening when Crackle and Tamara were allowed to leave Interview Room One at the police station. PC Billings was reluctant to let them go. But she had to get home to put her children to bed. She didn't know which of them she found the most despicable, Crackle for his martyred protestations of innocence, or Tamara for her mindless worship of Crackle. PC Billings thought she would go mad if she ever heard the phrase 'She fell out of her cot' again.

She had often felt murderous towards her own children, especially James, who whined in the day and wet the bed at night. Once, when he'd had a bad cold and she'd seen him surreptitiously wipe his nose on the sleeve of his clean school sweatshirt, she'd been so enraged that she had hit him hard on the side of his head, and knocked him off balance. She had found herself screaming at him, that if he wet the bed that night he would have to wash all his bed linen by hand.

She switched the recorder on to check the tape and heard Crackle say, 'You look shit in that dress; your belly sticks out,' and Tamara saying, 'I won't wear it again.' She then heard her own voice saying, 'Tamara, social services are going in front of a judge tomorrow morning to make Storme a ward of court.'

Tamara's voice on the tape sounded muffled. 'What's that mean?' Crackle shouted, 'It means the bastards will take our kid off us.'

'How long for?' said Tamara.

'For ever. If you stay with him you'll never get her back.'

'I didn't touch that kid!' said Crackle. 'She fell out of her cot!'

PC Billings turned down the volume knob and quietened the rest of his tirade, then turned it up again to hear Tamara say, 'I'm sorry Crackle, but I want the baby back.'

Crackle shouted, 'What you saying, Tam? You saying we're finished?'

'I'll go and live with dad until it's sorted,' she said, placatingly.

PC Billings heard herself say, 'Your dad's sobered up now. Go home with him and forget about this scumbag, eh?' Then the tape came to the end of its reel, and there was silence.

As PC Billings drove home she saw her ex-husband drive past her in his patrol car. He flashed his headlights in recognition and she flashed back.

Her son, James, came downstairs when he heard her key in the lock. She could see from the puffiness around his eyes that he'd been crying.

'You're late!' he shouted. 'You said you'd be home by eight o'clock, and it's ten past nine!'

Carole already had her coat on. PC Billings could tell by the set of her mouth that it wouldn't be long before she would have to advertise for another baby-sitter again. When she'd paid her and closed the door on her she took James upstairs and tucked him into bed. But he came downstairs three times, seemingly oblivious to her mounting anger. She gave him water, she escorted him to the toilet. For what seemed like the hundredth time that week she read *James and the Giant Peach* to him through half-clenched teeth, turning the pages with a crack. At eleven o'clock when he'd been in his bed for ten minutes, she ran a bath and lay in it in a stupor of tiredness. Then she heard his bedroom door open and his feet on the stairs, and his shrill cry from downstairs when he couldn't find her.

'Mummee! Mummee!'

As she got out of the bath and wrapped a towel around her, she wished that James had never been born. She pictured herself grabbing him by the lapels of his pyjama jacket, dragging him up the stairs, throwing him into the scented bath water and pushing his head under water until air bubbles stopped coming out of his mouth and nose. However, when she saw him, skinny and frightened, she drew him to her tenderly and promised that he could sleep with Mummy, again.

Thirty

Angela came to Christopher's house after work. He opened the door. She was still angry and wouldn't cross the threshold. She said, 'I didn't *kill* it, Christopher, it wasn't alive.'

'Of *course* she was alive,' he shouted. 'I felt her *move*, that Sunday.'

She had left her car in the middle of the road. The driver's door was open and the engine was still running. The interior light was on and Christopher could see that she'd been food shopping. There were two plastic bags on the back seat. A fresh pineapple poked out of one. Christopher couldn't take his eyes off the pineapple's fibrous leaves. It didn't belong in this snow-covered landscape, he thought. It wasn't natural. She shouldn't have bought the thing. It belonged in the tropics. It was inappropriate to have it here in this cul-de-sac with snow piled against the verges.

'I've got to go,' she said. 'Gregory's got wine appreciation tonight.'

'What's that got to do with *you*?' He was furious with her.

'I've got to cook his dinner before he goes out,' she said. She knew how feeble this must sound to him. A car pulled up behind Angela's car, and a young woman tapped impatiently on the steering wheel. Angela said, 'We take it in turn to cook dinner. It's my turn.'

'How can you cook for somebody you don't love?' shouted Christopher. The young woman, whose car Angela was blocking, sounded her horn and Angela went to her car and drove away without looking back. As she waited to turn on to the dual carriageway she glanced into her rear view mirror and saw that Christopher's front door had closed.

When she got home Gregory was at the stove, moodily stirring canned tomato soup in the saucepan she liked to use exclusively for milk.

'You know it's wine appreciation,' he said accusingly, as he lifted the saucepan off the stove and poured the soup into an earthenware bowl.

'Sorry,' she said, 'the snow made me late.' Then, 'Gregory, your *hair*!'

'The main roads are clear,' he said. 'I got home on time.'

His sideburns and the carefully constructed oiled waves he'd had for over twenty years had gone. His hair was now short and brushed away from his forehead. Without the darkening effect of hair oil she could see that his hair was almost entirely grey. He looked like a distant relation of himself.

'I feel like a new man,' he said.

At eleven a.m. Gregory had left the shop in the care of his assistant and strolled around the city centre inspecting hairdressing salons. He didn't want to go anywhere too radical. He rejected places with distressed paintwork and spotlights. He also spurned the old-fashioned barbers' shops where middle-aged men in white jackets imposed their views on their customers. Gregory had chosen the Upper Cut, a unisex salon where Ella Fitzgerald sang above the noise of the hand-held driers. Michelle, a senior stylist, gave him a consultation. He explained to her about wanting a new look. Together they settled on a style.

'We call it the Prussian schoolboy,' she said, and led him towards a wash basin where his hair was washed and conditioned by a junior called Zoë. In answer to her incurious enquiries about his arrangements for Christmas, he told Zoë about his childlessness, how Christmas wasn't the same without children, how he longed for a child, preferably a boy, to carry on Lowood's Linens. He told Zoë things he had never told Angela. To Michelle he confessed his fear of death. As his hair fell to the floor he talked about the black void waiting for him. Michelle told him that she wasn't too keen on death either, and didn't know anybody who was.

When she'd finished brushing and blow-waving, Gregory allowed himself to look directly into the mirror in front of him and was uplifted by what he saw. His head looked strong and manly; his features were more pronounced. When Michelle picked up a hand mirror and showed him the back of his head, he thanked her enthusiastically, saying, 'I hadn't realised what a good thick neck I've got.' He had left the shop to the mellow sound of Ella Fitzgerald singing, 'Mr Wonderful'.

'It makes you look older, Gregory,' said Angela.

'Good,' said Gregory, admiring himself in the hall mirror.

Fifteen minutes after Gregory had left the house, the doorbell rang. Angela looked through the fish-eye peephole in the front door and saw with horror that it was Christopher. She opened the door, but kept the security chain on.

'You've got to tell me, Angie,' he said desperately.

He put an arm through the door and grabbed at the material of the apron she was wearing. The apron strings which were tied at the waist tore, and Christopher lost his footing and almost fell.

'Go away, Chris, you shouldn't have come here!'

She was trying to close the door on him. She was terrified that Gregory would return and find Christopher on his doorstep.

'You've got to tell me about our baby. If she's dead, where's she buried?'

Christopher threw himself at the door. The chain broke and he was in the hall with the dog. He slammed the door shut and wiped his feet on the coconut mat which said: *Bienvenido*.

'I got a taxi,' he said. 'I can't keep away from you.'

He looked around the spacious hall. He recognised that the pattern on the wallpaper was William Morris. The handrail, banisters and newel posts of the dog-leg staircase had been burnished to a high reddish sheen. On the wall facing the front door there was a painting of Angela's mother and father. They were posed against the huge stone fireplace at Newton Harcourt; they were wearing evening dress, and looked at ease with themselves and their place in the world. There was an arrangement of winter flowers in a vase, on a polished table. Angela's car keys were in a Wedgwood dish. He could see into the kitchen at the end of the hallway. The pineapple stood on a chopping board on a work surface. She'd obviously got as far as cutting the top off before answering the door to him.

'You can't stay here,' she said.

'You can't stay here, either,' he said. He followed her into the gleaming modern kitchen.

Angela picked up a knife and resumed peeling the pineapple. A pool of juice collected on the chopping board. Christopher frowned at the pineapple and said, 'There should be a season for everything.'

She didn't know what he was talking about, and she was too panic-stricken to engage him in any further conversation. She longed for him to leave. He was as intrusive as a shard of metal in an eyeball. He wandered around the kitchen touching the laminated surfaces. The dog followed him; its paws made a desiccated sound on the vinyl tiles.

'Will you show me your garden?' he said. He knew how much she loved it.

'It's under snow,' she said. 'What's the point?'

'Please.'

'Chris, you've got to *go*. What if Gregory comes back?'

'I hope he does. I *want* him to know about us.'

'You're being cruel. It's not like you.'

She was crying and slicing through the pineapple, then lining a buttered Pyrex dish with the yellow rings.

'I know what *matters*, Angie.' He tried the door to the garden. It was locked. 'And in the scheme of things, bearing in mind infinity, Gregory's feelings really don't matter to me.' Christopher realised how awful this statement must sound to her, but he'd got this compulsion to tell the truth lately.

'Bearing in mind infinity,' she said angrily. 'What are you reading now? Patrick Moore?'

'No, Nietzsche,' he said. He stared her down, defying her to laugh.

'Gregory's feelings matter to me,' was all she said. She wiped her eyes on her apron. She was desperate for him to leave. It was inconceivable to her that Gregory could come home and find Christopher in the house. They had made the house their life. Every care and attention had been lavished on it. They subscribed to two interior design magazines. They were stacked in several piles on the bottom shelf of the bookcase in what they called, 'the family room'. Angela leaned against the draining board and wept helplessly.

'Don't cry, chick; I love you.'

He tried to put his arms around her again but she moved away and turned a switch above the oven which was set high in the wall. A red glow illuminated the interior, revealing gleaming, stainless steel racks.

'If you loved me, Chris, you'd go. You would. You don't know how frightened I am. I've got to make him a pineapple upside-down cake.'

Christopher laughed incredulously. 'Why?' he said.

'Because it's his favourite. Because I want a quiet life. Because I haven't given him any children,' she shouted. Christopher watched in silence as she slopped a soft sponge mixture on to the top of the pineapple circles, smoothed it with a spoon, and put in on the middle shelf of the oven.

'Tell me about our baby and I'll go,' he said. 'Tell me in the garden.'

She went to a key box on the kitchen wall and took a key off the hook labelled 'kitchen/garden door'. Before she could put the key in the lock the dog was at the door. As soon as it was open it ran across the garden dribbling yellow urine on the snow.

Angela went into the conservatory and put her quilted green coat on and stepped into her rubber gardening boots.

The garden looked like a brightly lit stage set. The security lighting showed the skeleton of every shrub and tree. The snow-covered lawn was like a white sea of phosphorescence. A rustic bench was upholstered in snow. Christopher cleared the snow from the bench with his hands, then scooped some together, compressing it into a hard ball. He then rolled it along the terrace and the ball grew quickly and seemed to take on a momentum of its own.

'Tell me about the baby,' he said.

Angela pulled a packet of cigarettes and a pink throw-away lighter out of her apron pocket and said, 'She weighed about two and a half pounds.'

Christopher rolled the ball into the middle of the lawn and patted snow around the base.

'Go on, I'm listening,' he said, with his back turned to her.

'You couldn't have called her pretty, Chris. But she was very wonderful. You can imagine, can't you, how the cave people felt when they looked up at the moon. You know, full of wonder. Well that's how I felt when I saw her. I shouldn't have *seen* her. I didn't want to. The thing is Chris, the thing is . . .' He was making a smaller ball now, his back was still turned. She couldn't see his face.

'There was a nurse in the room who hadn't seen a late-term abortion before and when our little one was born she got, well, emotional.'

Christopher turned around and placed the smaller ball on top of the larger. Making a featureless snowman.

'Emotional, why?'

'Because our little one was born with a pulse, Chris.'

Christopher rested his hand on the snowman's shoulder and looked at her.

'The doctor went out as soon as she was born. He'd missed a meal break he said, but I knew he despised me and couldn't wait to get away. He'd warned me that the labour would be painful, but I wasn't prepared. I wasn't brave, you see. I'll never forget that pain. I wish I could tell you how bad it was. Imagine somebody continuously tearing your body in half . . . I screamed for four hours solid. I had no voice when you came, remember?'

'I remember.'

'So they left me with this nurse.'

'What was her name, Angie?'

'Susan. So Susan was in charge of disposing . . . the thing is Chris, she couldn't do it. She should have put the baby in a container and put the container into a bag. But she couldn't do it, not while there was a pulse.'

Christopher tore two buttons off his overcoat and gave the snowman eyes.

'She lived for nineteen minutes. Susan and I watched her chest jerk up and down. Susan said that only one of her lungs was working, and then that stopped working.'

Angela lit another cigarette, then pressed the pink lighter into the snowman's face, making a forbidding slit of a mouth.

'She asked me not to tell anybody and I didn't.'

'Not even me,' he said.

'*Especially* not you.'

'Did you hold her, Angie?'

'Yes, I did. I held her. You can't imagine how tiny her hands were.'

'You told me some terrible lies, didn't you?'

'Yes, I did. I never thought I'd tell you the truth. I can't believe you know the truth now.'

She looked up at the black sky, expecting to see that the stars had gone. The world had entirely changed for her now that Christopher knew the truth about their baby. She felt light enough to float. They both looked at the snowman.

'We ought to give it a nose,' he said.

She went back into the house and opened the refrigerator door and took a carrot out of the vegetable crisper box. Then she went into the cloakroom in the hall and selected a red scarf and a blue and white striped bobble hat. She took these into the garden and gave them to Christopher and he finished dressing the snowman. When he stepped back to admire it, Angela looked at her watch and said, 'He'll be home in three-quarters of an hour. You said you'd go.'

But it was as if she hadn't spoken. He fiddled with the snowman's scarf and said, 'We'll have to find out where she is, Angie.'

'It's seventeen years.' She sat down on the bench and bowed her head, her hair swung slowly forward, completely obscuring her face.

'Somebody will know where she is,' he said. 'Finding her will give me something to do.'

He knew that this was the right time to tell Angela about the other one, the one he'd found in the ditch, but he knew that if he did tell her she'd be frightened of him. She would think he was mad and that would mean that they would never be together as man and wife.

Thirty-One

Gregory was disappointed to find that the wine appreciation class had been cancelled. There was a note on the door to the classroom they used which said, 'Cancelled due to the weather'. He had been looking forward to tonight. The tutor had promised to show them a video called 'Great Cellars of the World'.

Gregory was thinking about converting his own cellar at home into a wine store. The central heating boiler would have to be moved, and a few pipes diverted, but he felt it would be worth it for the pleasure of strolling along the racks before dinner each night, selecting something that went with the food. As he walked along the sixth form college corridors towards the exit, he wondered how many years it took before thick dust settled on a bottle. The tutor wore a brown overall in his own cellar, he'd informed the class. In his mind's eye Gregory saw himself climbing his own cellar steps whilst wiping the bottle clean.

As he left the warmth of the building and crossed the carpark towards his car, he tried to estimate how much racking he would need. He'd do all the work himself, he thought. No sense in paying a carpenter for such a simple job.

He stopped off at an off-licence on the way home, and spent ten minutes selecting a wine that would go with ham salad and pineapple upside-down cake. After careful deliberation he chose a £4.99 riesling which he felt would not swamp the flavours of the food.

Gregory let himself in and immediately noticed that the safety chain was broken. His first instinct was to shout Angela's name, but then he saw a dog, a bull terrier, come out of the kitchen and stand growling at the end of the hall. Gregory had never been that keen on dogs, but he was terrified of bull terriers. Weren't they the ones that savaged kiddies? He backed off and felt behind him for the handle of the front door. In seconds he was outside on the porch again.

Terrible images filled his mind. A burglar, a rapist. Angela tied up and defiled.

He listened intently but could hear nothing but the traffic passing at the top of the road. He unlocked the garage door and without switching on the light walked through it past the junk stored inside and into the garden.

He couldn't see at first, such was the glare of the lights on the snow. Then he made out three figures. One was Angela, one was a tall man, and one was a child in a white coat, red scarf and Gregory's own blue and white football hat. Because Angela and the tall man were embracing, it took Gregory some time before he realised that the small person in the white coat was a snowman.

As he watched the tall man pressing his mouth against Angela's mouth he felt as though a giant were treading on his chest. When the man undid her coat and stroked her breasts, Gregory retreated back inside the garage. It wasn't seemly to watch.

He leaned against his wooden workbench and tried to calm himself. He was surprised to find that his whole body was trembling with desire for his wife. He let himself out of the garage, and got into his car and drove to a petrol station, where he picked up a sack of logs from the forecourt. He then drove back home and saw the tall man and the dog crossing the road near his house. He drove around the block several times to give Angela time in which to compose herself, then he revved the engine noisily and parked outside their house.

He wondered how she would explain the snowman to him. He decided not to confront her with what he'd seen. The thought of listening to her lies thrilled him almost as much as the sight of another man desiring his wife's body. It was an affirmation that Gregory owned a prize.

Gregory smiled when he saw the clumsy repair that had been made to the security chain on the door. He went into the kitchen with the logs and the wine and found Angela stirring custard in a pan on the stove.

'You're just in time,' she said. The lights were out in the garden, but he could see the shape of the snowman through the reflection on the kitchen window.

She'd set the table for one. A plate of ham salad was ready for him.

'How was the class?' she said.

'Very good. We had a video, "Great Cellars of the World".'

He watched her face carefully as she poured the custard into a glass jug. Her lipstick was freshly applied. He wanted her badly. He took the sack of logs into the living room and lit a fire, using kindling already in the hearth, then cajoled it into life by blowing on the flames. He crouched in front of it until Angela called him through to the kitchen. She had opened the wine and had already drunk half a glass. He knew that she would drink heavily tonight, and he was glad. There were some things he wanted to tell her about himself and he didn't want her to be entirely sober when he did so. Before he sat down to eat, he filled her glass to the very top, then he ate in silence and watched his wife as she first inverted the Pyrex dish on to a dinner plate, then lifted it, like a conjuror, to reveal a perfect pineapple upside-down cake.

Thirty-Two

Angela couldn't get out of bed. She'd drunk most of the wine and a quarter of a bottle of vodka the night before. She burrowed her head in the pillow and made small whimpering noises. She could hear Gregory downstairs making tea. She could tell from the smell of the after-shave in the room that he had already showered, shaved and dressed. She turned her head slowly and squinted at the alarm clock on the bedside table; it was ten minutes past eight. She was going to be late for work again. She dreaded going into the agency and seeing the reproachful faces of the other workers.

Gregory came into the bedroom carrying two mugs of tea. He put one on the bedside table next to her, using the Stephen King novel he was reading as a coaster. She turned over and sat up in bed, then pulled the duvet up to cover her breasts when she realised that she was naked.

'There's a snowman in the garden,' said Gregory.

Her brain wasn't engaged yet. She couldn't remember what she had planned to tell him. Her wits were not yet sufficiently exercised by deception. To give herself time she picked up the mug and sipped the scalding tea.

'I built the snowman as a surprise, for you,' she said. Her tongue was burning from the tea. She interpreted this as a suitable punishment for a liar. Gregory handed the pink disposable lighter to her and said, 'Thank you, I've given him a more cheerful mouth, I stuck a piece of orange peel in.'

She badly needed a cigarette, but there was a rule that she wouldn't smoke in the bedroom.

'Can I, Gregory, just this once?' she said, reaching for a packet of cigarettes in her bedside drawer.

'Slut,' he said, but he was half-smiling. So she lit a cigarette and leaned her head against the pink, padded headboard.

'I might take the morning off,' she said. 'I feel terrible.'

'That's my fault,' he said. 'I wore you out last night, didn't I, slut? Didn't I, you fat, dirty whore?'

'Gregory!' she protested. She had never heard him use such language before, to her or to anyone else. He dragged the duvet off the bed, and threw it on to the floor. He kicked his shoes off and unbuckled the belt in the waistband of his trousers, and continued to call her 'slut', 'whore' and even 'harlot'. He removed his trousers and tartan boxer shorts and she saw that his penis was hard. There was nowhere to stub the cigarette out. She tried to roll off the bed, but he pushed her down and said, 'Smoke it, whore! Smoke it!'

Then he sprawled her legs apart, and pushed his erection inside her. It was painful and she cried out. Then he told her the things he had intended to tell her the night before. He was pleased now that she had fallen asleep in front of the fire. It would be far worse to hear such things in the marital bed in a cold north light.

'I'm going to tell you now, slut. I'm going to tell you about me and my women. I had my first affair two days after we came back from honeymoon. Marcia, remember Marcia. God she was gorgeous. Gorgeous. Her arse, Jesus!' Underneath him Angela tried to remember Marcia, but could only think of a snaggle-toothed woman who had once worked in the optician's next to Lowood's Linens.

'Then there was Mrs Daventry. You know Mrs Daventry, I had her at the back of the shop on top of a bale of towels, just after I'd closed up. She was tight and wet and I made her come three times.'

Angela did know Mrs Daventry. She was the linen buyer for a local chain of hotels, one of Gregory's best customers, but she was surely out of Gregory's league . . .

'And *so* many whores, every shape, colour, age, two whores a week. Pay them to dress up. Schoolgirls, nurses, French maids, women queue up for me. Rub against me in the shop . . .'

He was breathing heavily now and she knew that he would come soon.

'Tell me Angie,' he moaned, 'tell me about the men you've had, you whore, you slut.'

He had a picture in his mind of the tall man stroking Angela's breasts. He moved the picture on a frame and the man was sucking Angela's nipples, then Gregory lost everything. As he ejaculated, he shouted, 'Tell me!'

But Angela told him nothing.

As they dressed and washed, neither of them mentioned Marcia or Mrs Daventry, or the whores. Gregory put on his best overcoat and a Russian-style hat made of astrakhan. He went out and backed Angela's car out of the drive and parked it in the road. This gave him an excuse to study the interior of the car, but he found nothing to tell him the identity of the tall man with the dog. Before he came back into the house he dropped Angela's car keys down a drain. He wanted to make her suffer. She accepted his offer of a lift, and pretended to believe him when he claimed to have dropped the keys accidentally. They talked about their forthcoming holiday in Barbados during the journey into town, and kissed goodbye before Angela got out of the car.

When she got to work, there was a yellow post-it note, stuck to the computer screen on her desk. On it was written, 'Same place, usual time'.

The agency was busy all morning, the phone rang constantly with enquiries about late Christmas bookings, and people queued at the counters, desperate to get away from dreary England. The temperature had risen slightly in the night, and a thaw was under way; but the air was heavy with moisture and the ground was covered in dirty slush. Angela thought about Christopher constantly. She had told him the truth about the baby and he still wanted to see her. She vowed to make herself more beautiful for him.

All the time she was talking to customers she was thinking about leg waxing, pedicures and dyeing the grey in her hair. She kept making small mistakes and was constantly apologising.

Eventually she could bear the confinement no longer and announced to the girls that she was going out for an hour. She gave them no explanation, but as soon as she'd shut the door Claire said to Lisa, 'She's got a fancy man.'

Thirty-Three

Angela took her clothes off and hung them on a peg in the changing cubicle. When she was naked she looked at herself in the full-length mirror. The harsh fluorescent lighting overhead was merciless. It showed every discoloration of skin, every pucker of dimpled flesh.

'How can he love me?' she thought.

Then she thought, 'How can *they* love me?'

She turned her back on her own reflection and reached for the red satin outsized underwear she'd chosen with the help of an assistant. She disentangled the bra, the French knickers and the camisole from their fiddly little hangers. She was pleasantly surprised to find that they fitted perfectly. Still with her back turned to the mirror she took a red lipstick out of her bag and drew a cupid's bow on her lips. Then she brushed her hair, and only then when she was looking her best, did she allow herself to turn around and look at her reflection. 'Yes,' she said to herself.

She couldn't bear to re-dress in the sensible cotton underwear she'd been wearing when she entered the shop. She called the shop assistant guarding the entrance to the changing rooms, and gave her the satin things and cash which she'd drawn without Gregory's permission, from their joint account earlier. While she waited for the girl to return she tried to look at her naked reflection with more kindly eyes. Centuries earlier her voluptuousness would have been highly desirable she reasoned: paintings of women like her were admired in art galleries all over the world. The girl came back with her things and her receipt. As she re-dressed in her new underwear she thought about Christopher. When she met him in the café at lunchtime today she would tell him what she was wearing under her dowdy blue uniform.

Red used to be his favourite colour.

On the way back to work she was conscious of the satin gliding next to her skin. She looked into the faces of the middle-aged men and women she passed on the pavement and wondered if they had somebody to love them. She wished fervently that somebody would love Gregory one day, and that he would reciprocate this person's love. She dawdled past shop windows. Everything she saw she related to Christopher. She mentally refurnished his house from the Habitat window. She fantasised about buying a pair of brogues for him in Lilley and Skinner. In her imagination she fastened a Rolex watch costing £3,000 around his wrist. She understood why people in American musical films danced down Fifth Avenue singing about their love.

There was a sullen atmosphere in the agency when she got back. She'd been out longer than she'd said, and the girls behind the counter looked beleaguered as they faced the long queues in front of them. She tried to appease them by insisting that they each take a longer tea break than usual, but when Angela left for her lunch hour, the cold atmosphere between them all remained.

Her route from the travel agency to Veronica's Café led her past Woolworths. She walked automatically through the doors and approached the Pick 'N' Mix before remembering that she was wearing red satin underwear and would probably be having sexual intercourse with one man in the evening and perhaps another man at night. The thought made her sick with excitement and fear, and she turned her back on the cornucopian sweet counters and left the shop.

Thirty-Four

Ken was checking the weather from his bedroom window when he saw Crackle walking down the path towards the front door. Tamara was at the back of the house in the kitchen. Ken shouted, 'Tamara, don't answer the door.'

'Who is it?' she said.

'Him.'

'Oh.'

She didn't know how to explain to Crackle why she'd chosen the baby instead of him, so she ran upstairs and shut herself in the back bedroom, the one she had slept in as a child. Some of her toys were still there, lined up on the shelf. She sat on her narrow bed, closed her eyes, and listened to the doorbell ringing and ringing. Brandy barked frantically.

When the banging on the front door started, she took Jennifer, the doll whose eyelashes she'd once trimmed with nail scissors, down from the shelf and rocked her in her arms. Now that Tamara was grown up Jennifer felt cold and stiff and unfamiliar. She put her back on the shelf, next to Barbie in the wedding dress and Paddington Bear.

He was kicking at the front door now and shouting for her. 'Tamara, Tam, I know you're there. I got to talk to you.'

She went out on the landing and saw Ken at the top of the stairs. He had a duster in his hand, and was rubbing it automatically along the banister rail.

'Shall I just go and talk to him?' she said.

'Stay where you are,' Ken ordered. 'You're finished with him for good. You promised.'

Tamara nodded, but she knew that she would never finish with Crackle. She was his woman for life, his handmaiden. It didn't matter what bad things he did. He wasn't like ordinary people, he had been chosen by Satan to do Satan's work on earth. The day after their wedding she had asked him when Satan wanted them to begin this important work. For some reason he grew angry and said that there would be a sign one day.

She knew he was a crack head: that he would need to go to a crack house for a few days each week. But he'd got it under control, he said. Satan approved of crack: it was part of his plan to rule the world.

When the noise at the front door stopped, Tamara ran to the bedroom window and watched through a chink in the net curtain as Crackle stomped through the slush on the pavement. She longed to run down to him. He looked sad all on his own.

Ken saw her face and said, 'You'll get over him.' He didn't know that Tamara *belonged* to Crackle. Handmaidens had to stay with their men.

'What's going to happen then, Dad?' she said.

She wanted to know what was inside her dad's head. She followed him down the stairs, pausing occasionally when he stopped to dust the wooden treads on either side of the stair carpet. 'We'll try and get Storme back. We'll get a solicitor and do it properly. You'll grow your hair and let the blonde come back and I'll stop drinking and get a grip and go to work.' Tamara said automatically, 'And will we be happy ever after?'

Ken pulled Tamara towards him and tried to hold her. It was years since she'd allowed him to show any affection to her. He felt her stiffen with embarrassment, and he quickly let go of her again and went into the kitchen to put the kettle on, though tea was the last thing he wanted. There was a bottle of Johnnie Walker in the living room, next to the tropical fish tank, but he was going to the hospital to see Storme, and he couldn't turn up there drunk. Staff Nurse Fox had already had a go at him. He would just have to pray hard to Jesus and ask him to lessen the pain of being sober.

Tamara went into the living room, and switched the television on using the remote control. There was a satellite dish attached to the pebble-dashed front wall of Ken's house. He was able to receive eighty-seven TV channels. When he came into the room with the tea Tamara was pressing the plus sign of the remote control and working her way through all of the eighty-seven channels. The constant flickering of the screen annoyed Ken, but he kept quiet.

'There's nothing on,' she complained.

She eventually stopped at a shopping channel and watched an American woman in a leotard demonstrating a metal rocking device called 'A Tummy Trimmer' in front of a screaming studio audience. The woman had a figure so perfect that it looked moulded out of plastic. The camera closed in on the woman's face. She was smiling through unnaturally white, gritted teeth and saying, 'I'm *so* excited by this product.'

Tamara grew excited herself at the prospect of owning a Tummy Trimmer.

'I might get one of them,' she said to Ken.

'Why?' he said. 'You've got nowt on you.'

'I 'ave,' she said. 'I've got a belly lately.'

Ken looked at her thin ankles, showing beneath her black jeans. They reminded him of the bleached bones they had in glass cases in museums.

'Don't be so bleddy daft,' he said. 'You're nowt but skin and bone.'

'No, look, I *have* got a big belly.' She really wanted a Tummy Trimmer. She got to her feet and hauled up the folds of her baggy black jumper. The top button of her jeans was undone. The yellow zip was halfway down, and her belly was distended. Ken was surprised by the size of it. He said, 'You look pregnant.'

'I *told* you I'd got a belly.' Tamara laughed. 'Will you send for a Tummy Trimmer for me, Dad? I'll have it for Christmas, shall I? Then you won't have to go shopping.'

'But *why* is your stomach so big, Tam?' Ken couldn't understand why he hadn't noticed it before.

Tamara said, 'I dunno, but I can't be pregnant, I'm on the pill.'

'Then you ought to go to the doctor, that's not normal. Are you still having your monthlies . . . ?'

Ken was sufficiently worried to overcome his normal reticence about mentioning menstruation to his daughter. He had never acknowledged to Cath, his wife of twenty-one years, that she bled for a week every month.

Tamara tried to remember the last time she'd had a period: was it weeks, or was it months ago? She didn't take her contraceptive pills in the normal way. Crackle had told her that if she took a pill every day instead of for twenty-one days, she wouldn't have a period at all. Crackle hated his women to bleed; it was one of his things.

Tamara sometimes forgot her pill. She usually remembered to take two instead the next day to make up for it. She had only a sketchy idea of how anything worked, including her own body.

Ken went upstairs and had a wash and a shave, and changed into his second-best suit. When he looked into the living room, to tell Tamara that he was leaving to go to the hospital, she was still watching the

American woman who was now claiming that the Tummy Trimmer had changed her life for the better. Crackle had mentioned her big belly yesterday; that must have been the reason that he hadn't wanted sex or asked to see her dance naked for Satan, like he used to.

Thirty-Five

Early that morning Christopher went to the bank and requested to see his account manager, Lucca Fiorelli. He'd had letters from him describing the various specialist investment and insurance services the bank had to offer, but Christopher had never replied to his letters, or spoken to Mr Fiorelli on the phone. Everything had changed since Angela came back into his life. He would have to do something about money. He looked around. The banking hall was like a cathedral: there was stained glass, soaring ceilings and Victorian mouldings. He craned his head back and examined the painting on the domed ceiling: plump women draped in gauzy materials surrounded a pool on which lily pads and petals floated. He half-closed his eyes and pictured Angela, relaxed and smiling. Happy to be with women of her own kind. While he waited, he looked at the tiny photograph of Lucca Fiorelli in a brochure entitled 'Here to Help' which he'd picked up from a stand next to the seating area.

He read the writing under Lucca Fiorelli's handsome face. Apparently his account manager was the great-grandson of Italian immigrants. His great-grandfather known as 'the Okie Man' had sold ice cream from a customised three-wheeled bicycle. Fiorelli was quoted as saying, 'My great-grandfather was a good example of the small businessman's facility to resource the community.' Christopher frowned over this sentence: what did it mean?

Lucca Fiorelli put his head round his office door and said, 'Mr Moore?' He looked disapprovingly at the dog.

Christopher said, 'It's as good as gold.' The younger man hesitated a moment, then gestured that they were both to come in. His office had recently been refurbished. The walls were panelled in dark red mock mahogany. The room smelled of chemicals, like a dry-cleaner's shop. Fiorelli settled himself behind his paper-free, grey plastic desk and pressed buttons on a computer pad. He frowned at what he saw on the screen. 'You've had no movement on your accounts for over a year, Mr Moore; nothing in, nothing out. You haven't answered any of my letters.' He looked at Christopher, waiting for an explanation, but

Christopher couldn't think of how to explain to this young man in the sharp suit what his life had been like for the past year, so he remained silent.

'You asked to see me urgently. How can I help?' Fiorelli was bothered by Christopher's stillness.

'I want some money, please,' said Christopher.

Fiorelli laughed at the boldness of Christopher's statement. He said, 'I don't deal in overdrafts, Mr Moore.'

Fiorelli was forever anxious to detach himself from what he called, 'the dog'sbody work'. He liked to think of himself as being a creative financier. He was hungry for promotion. He had attended a course on body language at the weekend, and paid for it himself. Christopher said, 'I don't want an overdraft. I've got some first editions in a safe deposit box in this bank.'

'First editions of what?' asked Fiorelli.

'Books,' said Christopher.

'Oh, books,' said Fiorelli, unimpressed.

Christopher drew *Book and Magazine Collector* from his inside jacket pocket. Inside it, on a separate sheet of paper, was a list of the books in the safe deposit box. Christopher handed Fiorelli the sheet. He took it and frowned over the first title.

'*Erewhon?*' he said. 'What's that?'

'It's a novel by Samuel Butler, a first edition.'

'I don't have time to read novels,' said Fiorelli.

'That's a pity.'

'Is it?'

'Didn't you read novels at university?' asked Christopher.

'No,' said Fiorelli, 'I was too busy getting educated.'

He read further down the list. The only title he recognised was *Watership Down*; he'd seen the film. '*Watership Down*,' he said, aloud.

'It's worth two hundred and twenty-five pounds,' said Christopher. He found the relevant page in *Book and Magazine Collector*.

Fiorelli nodded, flicked at the list and said, 'So, what's your guesstimate of this lot then?'

'About five thousand pounds,' said Christopher. Fiorelli raised his eyebrows.

'Can I ask you what you've been living off for the past year?'

Christopher said, 'We've been living off my redundancy payment. It was in a building society, but it's all gone now.'

'We? You're married are you?' Fiorelli looked at Christopher's personal details on the screen. Under 'Marital Status' it said, 'Single'.

'By we, I meant me and the dog. I've got more valuable books at home,' he added.

'Have you got any more assets outside of this bank that I don't know about?' Fiorelli was getting interested.

'My house at Curlew Close belongs to me. I paid seventy-nine thousand pounds for it, a year ago, in cash. It's purpose-built for the executive lifestyle,' he said, quoting from the estate agent's brochure.

'Very nice,' Fiorelli said. He lived in a similar house.

'It's a horrible house,' said Christopher. 'Nobody's been born in it, and nobody has died in it. A year ago I didn't care where I lived. Now I do. I'm going to sell the house.'

'Things have changed have they?' Fiorelli prompted.

'Yes, everything has changed.' Christopher stood up. 'I need some money, today, right now.'

'I'll put somebody on to it for you, perhaps you'd like me to update your personal insurance, though, in view of your life changes?'

Christopher shook his head. 'No,' he said. 'There's no point. I won't die without her, and she won't die without me, and if you look on your computer again you'll find there's a trust fund already set up for the children. I did that in 1979.'

'How many children have you got, Mr Moore?'

'None yet,' said Christopher, clipping the lead on to the dog's collar and pulling it to its feet. 'So, if I go to the counter I can draw some money out, can I?'

Fiorelli said, 'Yes, go to the counter. I'll phone through. How much do you need?'

'I don't know,' said Christopher. Then he said, 'You know about foreign exchange rates. At current market prices, what would a Romanian baby cost me?'

Fiorelli laughed, picked up the phone and said to Christopher, 'No seriously, Mr Moore, how much do you need?'

Thirty-Six

Christopher found it was easier than he'd expected to see Storme again. He simply took the lift up to the seventh floor and went on to the ward and asked Staff Nurse Fox if he could see her.

'Are you a relation?' she asked.

'I'm her other grandfather,' he lied.

She appraised him quickly. 'She's asleep, don't wake her, she had a bad night.'

As they walked towards Storme's cubicle, Staff Nurse Fox wondered how such a well-dressed, softly spoken man could have produced a scumbag son like Crackle.

Storme looked clean against the white sheet she lay on. Somebody had cut her fingernails and her toenails, and brushed the wisps of hair showing underneath the dressings which covered most of her head. He noticed for the first time how long and dark her eyelashes were against her cheeks. It worried him that her body did not look at peace. Her limbs twitched occasionally, and her eyeballs moved under the closed lids.

'Do you think she's in pain?' asked Christopher.

'She's well sedated,' said the staff nurse, cautiously.

'Poor little chick,' said Christopher. He asked when she would be better.

'They're very resilient,' was all she'd say.

He wanted to see what she looked like when she smiled.

'Who else has been to see her?' he asked.

'Only her other grandfather,' said the staff nurse.

'Will her mum and dad be prosecuted?' he asked. He couldn't bring himself to say, 'My son.'

'I don't know,' she said.

'What will happen to her, when she's better?'

'I can't answer any of these questions,' she said, growing impatient with him. 'It's up to social services.'

'And the police?' he asked.

'Deliberate cruelty is difficult to prove. Babies can't talk,' she said.

'Perhaps she *did* fall out of her cot?' he tested.

'Perhaps,' she said, but he knew she didn't believe this, from the little downward movement she made with her mouth.

'Can I sit with her for a while?' he asked.

'No, I'm sorry, in the circumstances . . .'

'You think *I'll* hurt her,' said Christopher, angrily.

'It's Mr Parker-Wright's instructions,' she said, coldly. 'Her family can't be left alone with her.'

'Somebody should be with her all the time,' he said. 'She shouldn't be left. What if she wakes up and there's nobody here?'

'We're in and out of here all the time,' she said, stung by his inference that the nursing staff were neglecting Storme. She adjusted a catheter projecting from the baby's groin. 'We can't spare a nurse to sit with her for twenty-four hours a day. We're short staffed. She's well monitored,' she added. He looked through the window of the cubicle, down the corridor. Most of the cots and beds had an adult next to them, an Asian toddler with a leg in traction was surrounded by a phalanx of relations.

'I'm sorry, you'll have to go now,' she said.

Storme threw her right arm back and Christopher saw the name that was written inside the transparent plastic bracelet she wore on her wrist.

'Storme Natas.' He'd never known her surname. He waited for a moment to see if she would wake up, but her eyelids remained closed. He hoped that she was dreaming about an innocent world where there was no pain.

Staff Nurse Fox steered him out of the cubicle and down the corridor towards the lift. She wanted him off her ward. There was something about his intensity that made her uneasy.

The dog strained forward on its lead when it saw Christopher walk between the parting automatic doors at the main entrance to the hospital. It was hungry. Christopher had forgotten to buy a tin of dog food the night before, and the only food in the house was a packet of dried tortellini. They had shared this sparse supper in front of the gas fire in the living room: breaking the strict rule that the dog was only to be fed in the kitchen. Christopher needed company. He hadn't wanted to leave Angela behind in her coldly tasteful house.

He crossed the road separating the hospital from the café, and saw Angela in the far distance ahead of him on the pavement. She was wearing her little ankle boots, and was walking more confidently now that the snow had melted.

A smallish man wearing a navy cashmere overcoat and an astrakhan hat, slowed down on the opposite side of the road, and watched Angela go into Veronica's Café; he then walked away in the opposite direction. As the man in the hat passed them, the dog growled at him. Christopher said, 'Sorry,' and yanked the dog away. The man stopped and looked up hard into Christopher's face before hurrying away in the direction of the city centre.

Thirty-Seven

When Christopher arrived at Veronica's, Angela had placed a saucer on top of the cup to keep his tea hot.

'Let's go somewhere else,' he said. Angela was reluctant to leave the warm café where she felt safe, but he was insistent. As soon as they were outside on the pavement he embraced her. He took her arm when they crossed the roads. She knew she should have shaken him off. She'd been born in the city and so had he. Between them they knew hundreds of people. They were certain to be noticed by somebody. She said this to him and he frightened her a little by saying that he didn't care any more.

They walked towards the city centre and passed dangerously near to the market place and the Lowood's Linens shop. Christopher tried to put his arm around her waist, but she was too wide, and he contented himself with hanging his thumb on the decorative belt on the back of her overcoat.

'Where are we going?' she asked.

'We're going to spend the day together,' he said.

'I have to go back to work,' she said.

'This is more important than work.'

'I have to work, I need the money,' she said.

'I can get enough for two of us,' he said. He bent down and kissed the top of her head. She was reminded of her father taking two half crowns from his trouser pocket on a Saturday morning.

She said, 'I bought some new lingerie this morning. I'm wearing it now.'

'What's it like?' he said.

'It's red, and it's satin, not *real* satin.'

He pulled her off the pavement and into the doorway of a boarded-up shop. The dog stood sentinel on the slightly raised marble doorstep as Christopher pushed her against the door and opened the buttons of her overcoat. She pushed him away.

'Not here, Chris.' She struggled against him.

But his hand had already found a way through the layers of clothes to the satiny smoothness next to her skin.

'It feels lovely,' he said, and he pulled away slightly so that he could see as well as feel the red camisole she was wearing.

Gregory stopped outside a Car Phone Warehouse and looked across the High Street to where his wife and the tall man were kissing in a shop doorway, in daylight, in the middle of town. He took a small disposable camera out of his pocket and took three photographs of them. He needed concrete evidence: he didn't altogether trust his own eyes. This morning when he had woken up with Angela beside him he'd sought desperately to find an explanation for the scene he'd witnessed in the garden last night. Was the tall man a long-lost brother, reunited with the sister he'd never met? It was just possible, but did long-lost brothers crush their lips into the mouths of their newly found sisters? Gregory knew they did not. Still he'd given her something to think about this morning. He'd punished her by telling her about those other women.

Angela's face was pressed against Christopher's scratchy tweed over-coat. She noticed that he had already replaced the buttons he had torn off the night before. Angela turned her head and read '30,000 sq metres of Retail Space To Let' which was written on an estate agents' window. The town is dying, she thought.

Over the road Gregory took one more photograph before moving away, and because there were twenty-four more possible photographs left on the film, he continued to snap away at the city centre: the clock tower, the McDonald's restaurant; the market stalls and the grinning stall-holders; and the concrete Market Cross and its wino regulars with their squashed noses and red eyes. He was anxious to get the film developed that same day. He needed proof other than his own eyes that his wife was seeing another man. The last photograph he took was of his own shop. He posed his black assistant, Lynda, in front of a tower of white bath towels, for the contrast.

Christopher took Angela to Pasta's, an Italian restaurant in an area called St Kevin's Square, a new development of shops and up-market eating places. Genuine old buildings had been knocked down so that fake old buildings could be erected in their place. There was a bandstand in the middle of a small square where the Salvation Army played at Christmas and buskers licensed by the Council played throughout the rest of the year.

Christopher tied the dog to the bandstand under the apprehensive eye of a young man in a clown's costume who was about to juggle three clubs whilst riding on a unicycle. When they had been seated at a table by the window by an authentic-sounding Italian waiter, Christopher said, 'I hope you still love Italian food.'

Angela laughed nervously and said, '*This* is *mad*, Chris. I've only got ten minutes before I have to be back at work.' He handed her the huge menu and said, 'You're not going back to work this afternoon. You're coming with me to find out where our Catherine is.'

'I'm here.' Catherine sat down next to Angela and cricked her neck around to read the menu.

'Have the garlic bread, Mum; then I can have some.'

Angela smiled at Catherine and couldn't resist adjusting the collar of her white shirt, smoothing it down over her navy blue uniform cardigan. Catherine playfully tapped her mother's hand away.

'Mum, I'm not a baby.'

Angela said, 'I'll have some garlic bread, but I can't manage anything else, Chris.'

Catherine was laughing at the young clown's ham-fisted attempts to manage the unicycle and the clubs.

'What a saddo!' she said, then her own laughing face became sad as the clown fell off the unicycle yet again.

'He's not very good, is he?' said Angela.

'He's probably been on one of those poxy government training schemes for clowns,' said Christopher. Angela and Catherine laughed, and Christopher said, 'You think I'm joking, Angie. I'm not. We'll soon have more trained clowns in this country than trained engineers.'

Angela laughed again and held Catherine's hand under the table. Her daughter's hand felt exquisitely soft. Is this what it's like to have a family? she wondered to herself. She looked at Catherine's flawless complexion and thought to herself how lucky she was to be the mother of such a beautiful child. It wasn't only her looks she admired: she had won every sporting and academic prize open to her. Angela was so proud of her daughter.

She felt Catherine pull her hand away and when she turned the girl had gone, without saying goodbye.

Thirty-Eight

They walked in pouring rain to the railway station, where a long line of taxis waited for passengers under a glass-fibre roof. The driver of the first taxi in line was playing cards on the front of his cab with another driver. When Christopher approached him and gave him the address of the nursing home, he frowned and addressed his fellow drivers in Hindi. They conferred in Hindi for some moments while Christopher and Angela waited. Then, the first taxi driver said in English, 'It will be a lot of money. Leamington Spa is many miles.'

Christopher said, 'That's all right, I've got a lot of money.'

The driver then said, 'Please, the dog is not allowed to sit on any seat. This taxi is a London cab, only three weeks old.'

Christopher ordered the dog to lie on the floor with such ferocity that for the first few miles of the journey it lay as still as a stone dog, not daring to move.

Christopher and Angela held hands on the back seat and watched in silence as the town gave way to rainy suburbs and then to flooded countryside: they passed swollen brown rivers and ditches and once, to the driver's excitement, they were forced to take a diversion to avoid a flooded road under a railway bridge. The taxi seemed to be driving under water. A tractor carrying bales of hay made its way slowly towards them, the tyres half-submerged in the flooded field.

Angela tried not to watch the meter which changed with horrific frequency from pence to pounds. When it reached thirty pounds she whispered, 'Chris, the meter.'

He squeezed her hand and said, 'I've got money today, and this is how I want to spend it.'

They passed through a small village, where mothers waited under umbrellas outside an infants school.

The nursing home had hardly changed at all. The elm trees lining the drive had gone and been replaced by deadened green conifers. As the taxi crunched along the gravel drive Angela looked up at the small, dark-paned window of the room she had spent three days in before emerging to live her life as a childless woman. She knew that this journey was wasted. They would never find where Catherine was laid to rest. It was all so very long ago. She said none of this to Christopher, who was leaning forward eagerly on his seat, like a child on a trip to the seaside waiting for his first glimpse of the distant sea.

Christopher paid the driver, then persuaded him to wait for them, arguing that he was unlikely to get a fare for the return journey. The driver looked at the forbidding façade of the nursing home and the misty fields surrounding it and agreed to wait.

The rain had stopped. They walked the dog around the grounds and waited while it squatted at the side of a hedge. Angela was reluctant to go inside the building. She still remembered the sounds and the smells that had invaded and disturbed her thoughts for years after her two visits here. She still remembered the pain. They stopped and looked at the red-brick walls, the turreted roofs and the chimney stacks. Smoke escaped from one chimney pot. The taxi driver agreed that the dog could sleep on the floor of the cab. Then Christopher looked at his watch and said, 'It's time we went in.'

They walked across the staff carpark. In the area marked 'Doctors' Cars Only' stood two cars, a pale blue Bentley and a dark green Jaguar XJS. Christopher stroked them as he passed by and said, 'I see the murderers are at their work.'

They watched a mini-bus draw up to the steps by the porticoed main entrance. The driver, a young man in a dark business suit jumped out and went to the back of the van and opened the doors and pulled down a set of collapsible steps. Four women got out, each holding a small overnight bag. The driver held out his hand to help them down the steps. Each woman touched his hand briefly to aid her balance. The driver led them into the entrance hall and left them at a counter, like a hotel reception desk. Christopher and Angela followed, and waited their turn. The woman behind the counter wore a medical type uniform and a badge on her breast which said, 'Mrs Forsythia Oxenbury – Elms Nursing Home'.

Each woman gave her surname in a quiet voice: Cartwright, Taylor, Smith, Leystone, then stood back. Angela imagined the tiny floating things each woman carried in her womb. When the women had been processed by Mrs Forsythia Oxenbury and taken to their beds, Christopher told Mrs Oxenbury that he had an appointment to meet the owner of the nursing home, Mr Porteous De Lavery. This was news to Angela, but nothing he did surprised her now.

They waited for ten minutes, before being shown by Mrs Oxenbury into what looked like a private lounge. A coal fire burned in a grate. Porteous De Lavery was a small, polished man, whose greying hair was carefully arranged in strands across his head. He got up from the sofa and came towards them, smiling.

'Mr Moore?' he said. His voice was light and pleasant.

'And this is Mrs Lowood,' said Christopher. She saw De Lavery's glance of dismissal. A fat uninteresting woman, it said, though well enough dressed.

'I didn't quite understand what you wanted to see me about when you rang . . . please, do sit down.'

Christopher and Angela sat side by side on the chintz-covered sofa, and De Lavery sat in a leather armchair next to the fire. He crossed his small legs and turned towards them still smiling. Christopher said, 'Seventeen years ago our daughter was born here.'

De Lavery frowned and uncrossed his legs. 'Can I stop you there Mr Moore? This is not, and never was a maternity hospital.'

'I know that,' said Christopher, 'but, as I *said*, our daughter, Catherine, was born here on June 20th, 1979 at – what time was it, Angie?'

'Twenty to five in the afternoon,' she said quietly.

'She lived for about twenty minutes,' said Christopher.

'Then there should have been a birth certificate *and* a death certificate issued,' said Mr De Lavery. 'Was there?'

Angela shook her head.

'I'm not bothered about the *paperwork*,' said Christopher, 'but I would like to know where our daughter is.'

'I don't know what you mean by *is*, Mr Moore. Are you talking in the religious sense?'

Christopher laughed. 'Would I come to you if I wanted a discussion about heaven and hell? I've got shelves full of theology at home. Just now I'm half-way through St Thomas Aquinas.' Mr De Lavery was not a reader and was baffled by this turn in the conversation.

Angela said, 'Is she buried somewhere?'

Mr De Lavery got up and stood with his back against the fire. 'No,' he said. 'We ran out of consecrated ground in 1976.'

'So, what did you do with our little one, Mr De Lavery?' said Christopher.

'The . . . foetuses are incinerated, Mr Moore.'

'Whereabouts?'

'At the medical incinerator. The Waterloo Road Crematorium.'

'They're just thrown in, are they, in a bag?'

Mr De Lavery turned and kicked the coals in the grate. Red sparks flew up the chimney. 'Yes, they *are* just thrown in, in a bag. What would you expect us to do with them?'

Christopher took the question seriously. He thought for a moment, then turned to Angela and said, 'Did you think about it, Angie, at the time?'

'No,' she said. 'I just wanted rid of her, Chris.'

Mr De Lavery smiled gratefully at Angela, and went to the door and opened it. And as there was no more to be said, they thanked him and allowed him to show them out.

He watched until their taxi had turned the corner at the bottom of the drive, then went back to his room and warmed himself by the glowing coals of the fire. He should have remembered, he thought, to tell them that the incinerator was blessed annually by certified churchmen of various denominations. It might have given them a little comfort.

Later, as he made a short cut to his private apartment in a wing of the house, he passed by the operating suite. He stopped at the door of the recovery room and looked in. Women lay on their sides on high trolleys. Each had a stainless-steel bowl next to her head in which to vomit. Some were still sleeping, but of those awake, all were crying. It was only the effect of the anaesthetic, he knew that, but he found it particularly disconcerting today. He made a mental note to speak to the senior theatre nurse and ask that in future the door to the recovery room be kept closed.

Thirty-Nine

Gregory could hardly wait for the hour it took to develop the photographs to be over. He filled it by going back to the shop and arranging his Christmas lines. Putting boxed sets of tablecloths and napkins across a counter in a fan-like arrangement and sticking notices saying 'Gift Idea' on more or less everything. In the napery section he found the cardboard box that contained the Lowood's Linens Christmas decorations. He took out last year's nativity advent calendar, which was still in good condition, and opened the cardboard flap marked with the number one. A star, improbably yellow and surrounded by many dazzling beams of light was pictured inside. Gregory drawing-pinned the calendar above the cash till, next to a yellowing list of numbers of counterfeit £20 notes, supplied to him by the police. Between customers Lynda and he together with Betty, whom he'd inherited from his father and who helped him out at busy times, decorated the little shop, criss-crossing the ceiling with paper garlands and surrounding the shop window with twinkling fairy lights. When they had finished Gregory stood outside on the pavement and looked inside. 'It could be Santa's grotto,' he said to Betty.

'Except there's not a bleddy queue to get in,' she said.

Gregory wished he could ask Betty to retire permanently. Her cackling laugh and loose dentures lowered the tone. He only kept her on out of respect for his father. He put his overcoat, hat and gloves on and walked through the market to the store to collect the photographs he'd taken earlier in the day.

Ken was in the same store looking for pregnancy testing kits. He had never seen one. He only knew of their existence from reading the problem pages of the *Daily Mirror*. He prowled around the shelves of women's things, baffled by the sheer number of goods on display. Then, by a process of elimination, by understanding that the creams and gunk that they put on their faces and hair were separated from their medical stuff, he tracked down what he wanted. It was called 'Predictor'. He took his reading glasses from the top pocket of his jacket and put them on and read the back of the 'Predictor' packet. It promised completely accurate results. He would have to persuade Tamara to give him some of her wee somehow, but he would think how to do that on the journey home. As he made his way to the cash desk he saw the Estée Lauder soap, talc and bath-cube gift set he bought for Cath every Christmas. He bent and sniffed at the display and Cath's smell overwhelmed him for a moment, but he straightened his back and joined the queue and waited to pay.

Gregory was upstairs killing time by looking at the educational toys. He had already presented his ticket at the photography department counter, and had been told by a Chinese girl assistant to return in five minutes. He moved along the shelves until he came to a section labelled, 'pocket-money toys'. He picked up a kaleidoscope and held it to his eye, and was enchanted by the lustrous colours and multiplicity of patterns it contained. Gregory was impressed that it took only a slight turn of the metal tube for the luminous interior to regenerate itself into an entirely different multi-faceted world.

He took a wire basket from the stack next to the escalator and put the kaleidoscope inside. Why shouldn't he buy toys for himself, he thought. He didn't remember having many as a boy, and the few he did have, the train set and the lead soldiers, he was always having to tidy away. He bought himself two glove puppets, a monkey with a face that made him laugh, and a dog with a lolling left tongue. He bought a Scuba Diver Action Man, a Barbie Doll in a wedding dress and Ken her boyfriend in top hat and tails. Once started, he couldn't stop. He bought a battery-driven robot, a baby doll that wet herself, and a Hornby model train. Two metres of track, a railway station and, inside a bubble pack, a station-master, a guard and two porters. The woman at the toy department check-out asked him how many children he had. 'Three,' he said. 'Two boys and a girl.' Then, burdened by two carrier bags and the bulk and length of the train set, he collected the envelope of photographs from the Chinese girl.

He sat down in the pedestrian precinct, on a wooden bench outside the shop, settled his parcels and bags around him and opened the envelope. He sorted through them quickly, until he came to the three he'd taken first. His wife was in each photograph, as were the tall man and the dog. They were in the doorway of the shop, but, bafflingly, in each photograph there was another person. A beautiful dark-haired adolescent girl, wearing the uniform of one of the city's premier girls' schools. Gregory *knew* there had been nobody else in the doorway when he took the three photographs of his wife and the tall man. There had obviously been a mistake made during the processing. Somehow an image of a schoolgirl with a dazzling smile had been superimposed on to his own photographs.

He struggled back into the shop and told the Chinese girl in the photography department that they had ruined his photographs, thanks to 'their sloppy developing procedures'. The departmental manager, a Mr Crow, came from behind a door marked 'Staff'. He introduced himself and asked how he could help Gregory. Gregory informed Mr Crow that unless he received a new disposable camera and a gift voucher as compensation for his ruined photographs, he would be taking him to the Small Claims Court, once Christmas was over.

Mr Crow looked down at the photographs which were causing all the trouble. He couldn't work out what the silly sod was going on about. The photographs were a family group: the lovely girl in the uniform had her mother's hair and eyes, and her father's mouth and slim build. The three of them were beautifully framed in the shop doorway. The quality of the film was very good. No way was he going to give the nutter in the stupid hat anything at all. Eventually, after Gregory grew louder and more insistent in his complaints, Mr Crow rang security and Gregory was escorted from the premises by a silent security guard.

Forty

Ken locked himself in the bathroom and unfolded the instruction sheet from inside the 'Predictor' box, and studied it carefully. It was all simpler than he'd expected: all he needed to do was to dip the device into some of Tamara's wee and wait eight minutes, and if a blue ring appeared it meant she'd be carrying a baby inside her; Crackle's baby. He sat on the side of the bath and put his hands together and prayed fervently that she wasn't pregnant, that her belly was big due to other physical causes. She didn't know how to look after a baby, she was still a baby herself. It was him and Cath who'd looked after Storme for the first three months, before Tamara and Crackle had found a flat. Once, when he'd taken Cath on an outing to Drayton Manor Park with the church, they'd returned home to find Storme screaming with a burnt mouth: Tamara had warmed the baby's bottle in the microwave and hadn't checked the temperature. It was Cath and Ken who had sat up all night with Storme, spooning ice-cold sterilised water into the little scalded mouth.

It was a terrible day when Tamara and Crackle took Storme away to live in the flat. At first Ken and Cath visited twice a week, taking food and nappies and baby clothes. They played with the baby and tried not to comment on the thick crust of yellow scurf on her head, or the rank smell of her clothes. Cath took the baby's clothes home to wash and brought them back, sweet and clean, the next time. Sometimes Ken and Cath stood outside the front door to the flat listening to Storme crying inside. On one occasion when nobody had answered the bell, Ken had booted the door and shouted so loudly that the neighbours in the adjacent flat had come out and complained about Crackle and Tamara. They told Ken that they were sick of the noise they made: the kid was always crying, and the stereo was on so loudly that their walls vibrated. Tamara had eventually answered the door. She had sleep in her eyes, and was wearing Crackle's denim shirt and a pair of black knickers. Ken was disgusted to see that her neck and shoulders were disfigured by liver-coloured love bites. She stood on the threshold in bare feet and took the food and the freshly laundered baby clothes, but she was nervous and didn't want to let them in. They had pushed by her anyway. There was broken glass on the floor of the living room, and the television screen was shattered. Cath had said, 'See to the baby, Tamara, I'll clean this up.'

Ken had asked if Crackle was still in bed, and Tamara had started to cry and said, 'No, he's not been home for two days.'

In his absence Ken and Cath cleaned the flat and fed Tamara and Storme. They begged her to bring the baby and come home with them, but Tamara said repeatedly, like a mantra, 'No, I've got to be here when he gets home.'

At her request Ken had rung all the hospitals, secretly hoping that he would be told that Crackle was dead. Ken thought that he would volunteer to identify the body: it would give him great satisfaction to see that moronic bastard on a mortuary slab. But within four months it was Cath's body he was looking down on, not believing, despite the evidence of his own eyes, that this woman that he loved so passionately could be dead and gone from him for ever. He was only fifty-two. How could he live the rest of his life without her?

It was easy to get a sample of urine from Tamara. He told her that the community nurse was testing for diabetes, and had left a self-testing kit. Tamara believed him. She believed everything that she was told. Ken had finally admitted to himself that she was a stupid girl. They had called it 'learning difficulties' at school. There had been talk about sending her to a special school, but Ken had seen the mini-bus full of special-school children as it did the rounds of the estate in the early morning, and he fought to keep her out of that bus. Cath and he had tried to teach her to read and write at home, but each kitchen table session ended in frustration and angry tears. When she was older, she got by in the world because she was pretty – until she met Crackle, who had sucked all the prettiness out of her.

Ken added the urine to the padded device, and put it high up on top of the bathroom cabinet where Tamara wouldn't see it. He looked at his watch and noted the time. Soon he would know if she was carrying another baby inside her. He would fill the time by preparing to visit Storme. He took his shirt off and washed and shaved. As he rinsed the shaving foam from his face he looked at himself closely in the mirror and saw that he was turning into an old man. He couldn't remember the last time he'd smiled.

Ken forced himself to go downstairs and watch television. Tamara had possession of the remote control and maddened him by flicking from channel to channel. She lay full length on the sofa, her belly seemed more prominent than ever. A gathering of soft-drink cans and dirty cups stood on the floor within her reach. She'd been using a toast-crumbed plate as an ashtray. A haze of cigarette smoke drifted across the room from the slight draught he had caused by opening the door.

'Have you phoned the hospital about Storme?' he asked.

'I couldn't get through,' she said, keeping her eyes on the television, but he knew by the way her finger went to her mouth that she was lying. In her slothful state she had forgotten about Storme. She was not natural, thought Ken, and he prayed once again that the ring would not have turned blue when he went back upstairs.

Forty-One

Crackle swore when he saw the queue outside the prison visitors' centre. He hated queuing and would normally push to the front of any queue and ignore anybody brave enough to protest. But this queue was different. There were hard men in it, men to whom violence was a daily occurrence, and some of the women had faces that spoke of fighting and confrontation.

Crackle took his place behind a thin woman with extravagantly ringleted blonde hair, who was holding the hand of a small boy with a raw face and a shaven head. The boy was clutching a large picture he had painted at school. In Crackle's opinion the kid had laid the paint on too thick: different coloured flakes of it kept floating to the floor. Crackle could still remember the creamy smell that drifted up to him when he mixed the paints at junior school, and the delight in assembling the thick brushes and the sugar paper, and that moment, that fucking brilliant moment, when you made the first brush stroke on the paper. He read the name on the back of the painting. It was written in a teacher's neat italic hand. 'Grant Lee'.

Crackle was curious to see what kind of picture Grant had painted, but the kid kept waving it about, which irritated him. Then, as the queue moved along, Grant dropped the painting and Crackle saw that the picture was one that he himself had painted at school. A house, a path, a fence, a tree. And, at the side of the house, his real mum and his real dad and himself.

Crackle swallowed hard, and felt the weight of those heavy tear-shaped rocks inside him again.

After being searched by a prison officer and being sniffed at by an addicted Alsatian dog, hungry for drugs, Crackle was allowed into the visiting room. He sat down at a chipped Formica table. He kept his eye on the door that the prisoners entered by. He could hear Grant talking excitedly to his mother at the next table.

The room quickly filled up with visitors; there were defeated-looking middle-aged parents, young women who'd made a special effort to look glamorous, and other women who'd given up. There were young men who lounged back in the plastic chairs with their legs splayed defiantly, whose eyes were never still.

Crackle felt better about everything as soon as he saw Bilko come into the room, tall and black and handsome in his white t-shirt and jeans.

'You look good, man,' he said.

''S'all the sleep, man,' said Bilko. 'There's fuck-all else to do, innit? You look shit,' he added, censoriously, looking at Crackle's bluish-looking scalp and sunken face.

Crackle told Bilko his latest problem. How he had social services and the police on his back now because Storme had fallen out of her cot.

Bilko frowned. He liked children. He had four of his own. 'That's bad,' he said.

When Crackle told him that Storme had a fractured skull and that her spleen had been ruptured he said, 'Fuck, man. How'd you let that happen? She gonna be all right?'

'I dunno, the bastard doctor won't let me or Tam see her.'

Bilko thought about the time his eldest kid, Zachary, had drunk bleach. He hadn't left the kid's bedside for two days. He didn't remember even going for a piss.

'So they're saying *you* done it?' checked Bilko.

'Yeah, the *bastards*.'

Crackle's indignation was genuine. He hadn't *meant* to do her any damage. It was just that he wouldn't stand for her crying in the night. She had to learn that she couldn't get her own way.

'Do you swear to me that you *din't* do it, man?'

'Would I do that to my own kid?'

'You're too hard on her, man.' Bilko was troubled. 'I've seen how you give her big, big licks.'

'She gets out of hand sometimes,' said Crackle. 'She's not good like your kids are.'

'I don't give my kids *no* licks never, and neither does their mothers. It ain't right, Crackle. We're big and they're little, y'know?'

Crackle shifted uncomfortably on his plastic chair. He hadn't come here to be lectured.

'She was all right when she was a little baby, but as soon as she started walking she was a fucking nightmare. Always touching things. She did my head in!'

'Then you shouldn't have never had her!' shouted Bilko. The prison officers who were placed around the room looked across to where Crackle and Bilko were sitting. Bilko lowered his voice. 'All kids fuck about with things, Crackle. You gotta give 'em something else to do. I never saw you play with Storme, not once, 'an she was always shit up, y'know. If my kids was ever dirty like she was I'd give their mothers serious grief, y'know.'

Crackle said, 'Tamara's an idle cunt. She don't clean up or nothing, and anyroad we ain't got your money, Bilko.'

Bilko raised his voice again. 'How much is a fucking bar of soap?'

Heads turned.

Crackle answered, 'I dunno.' He had never bought a bar of soap. Soap was either there or not there.

'It's fucking *nothing*,' shouted Bilko. 'And why have I got money? Because I go out and I *hustle* for it! I work a fourteen-hour day, seven fucking days a week!'

A prison officer strolled over to the table where Crackle and Bilko were sitting turned away from each other.

'You got a problem here, Bilko?' he said.

'No,' said Bilko, turning and smiling up at the prison officer. 'Nothink I can't handle, Dave.'

'Yeah, well keep it down, will you?'

The prison officer patted Bilko on the shoulder and walked over to the refreshment stall where elderly ladies in green overalls were selling junk food and watery beverages to the prison visitors.

'Do you want anything?' asked Crackle, who wanted a change of conversation.

'Yeah, I want my kids,' said Bilko. He longed to hold them to him and listen to the strange funny things they said to him. They made him laugh more than any comedian ever did. Bilko looked away and watched Grant Lee talking to Craig, his dad. Craig was serving seventeen years for slicing a love rival's nose open with a beer glass, before setting fire to the man's flat. Bilko looked at Grant's shaved head and earrings in disgust. His own children attended a Church of England school and wore a uniform and polished shoes. You would never have known from looking at them (and Bilko prayed that they would never find out) that their father, he, Bilko, had a gun hidden inside the front passenger seat of his black BMW. None of them knew he was in prison. He phoned them every afternoon after school, and when they asked him why he didn't come home, he told them that he was in another country, which was almost true.

Bilko said, 'Crackle, don't come and see me no more, man.'

'Why, what I done?'

'You *know* what you done.'

And Bilko got up and gestured to Dave, the prison officer, that he wanted to go back to his cell. Bilko preferred solitude to keeping company with a man he knew for sure had harmed a child.

Crackle left the prison in a daze. As he walked towards Veronica's Café, he saw a blue illuminated sign on a church. 'Jesus Loves You,' it said.

Crackle stopped, and read the sign over and over again. He didn't know where to go after he'd been to Veronica's; he didn't want to go back to the flat. He didn't like it there without Tamara and Storme, and he didn't feel safe in the city no more, not without Bilko's protection. He'd got too many enemies and he was sick of waiting for a signal from Satan. He read the sign one last time before turning away. 'Jesus Loves You.' 'I'm glad some fucker does,' he said out loud. He looked around to see if anybody had heard him, but, as usual, there was nobody near to him.

Forty-Two

When Gregory got back to the shop he rang Heavenly Holidays and was told that Angela had rung in to say that she wouldn't be back at work in the afternoon. He spoke to Lisa, who acted as Angela's deputy in her absence. 'She's not been herself, lately,' said Gregory, defensively, after listening to Lisa's catalogue of complaints against his wife. Apparently, the worst of these was that Angela had booked a family of twelve on to a charter flight to Tenerife that had been taken off the timetable a year ago. Lisa had been forced to ring Head Office for authorisation to book the irate family into an airport hotel until seats on scheduled flights could be arranged for them.

'Will she be in tomorrow?' said Lisa. 'She's got three dirty mugs on the draining board in the staff kitchen.'

Gregory admitted that he didn't know what Angela's movements were tomorrow. He could hear telephones ringing in the background and a masculine voice raised in argument. Lisa said, 'I've got to go. Tell her to ring me.'

During the short time Gregory had been on the telephone a queue of women had built up at the cash till. His own Christmas rush had begun. The first woman in the queue had brought back a tablecloth she'd bought the day before, complaining that there was a design fault all over it. She pointed at the reindeer pulling Santa's sleigh, which ran as a continuous pattern around the edge of the cloth.

'Look, their antlers are faulty,' she said.

Gregory looked closely and saw that each right-hand antler was missing some brown thread, giving the reindeer a peculiar lop-sided appearance. The woman prodded a slim finger at the cloth. 'It's an authentic design,' said Gregory. 'In the wild you would never see a reindeer with identical matching antlers.'

'What utter nonsense,' she said.

He recognised from the woman's accent and self-confident manner that nothing but a full refund would satisfy her. He took £9.99 from the till and handed it to her with a smile, saying, 'And a Merry Christmas, madam.'

When she'd left the shop he went through the huge stock of reindeer and Santa tablecloths and found, to his profound horror, that each one had exactly the same design fault. He was on the telephone to his Portuguese supplier at once, but the person in the office who spoke English was out. He slammed the telephone down angrily, and, as was customary for him on occasions like this, practised telling Angela about his frustrating afternoon. Then he remembered that he couldn't be sure if Angela would be there when he got home, or if she would want to listen to him if she was.

He hoped that this stupid fling she was having was caused by the menopause. He'd read that some women changed their personalities for a while until their hormones calmed down.

Angela had once left him for two days and gone to stay in a hotel in Cromer. They'd had a quarrel about the correct way to stack the dishwasher, which had quickly escalated into a screaming row about money.

He still remembered the desolate atmosphere in the house after she'd gone. He hadn't known what to do with himself. Without her he felt incomplete.

Forty-Three

The rain had stopped. It grew dark on the journey back to the city. The moon and the sun were in the sky at the same time. Then the sun disappeared and it was only the moonlight that was reflected in the flooded fields. Christopher had closed the sliding glass window which divided the driver from them. They could tell by the way his shoulders slumped as he drove away from the nursing home that this gesture of separation had offended him. Christopher and Angela clung to each other on the back seat of the taxi, sliding along the shiny seat whenever the driver took a sharp corner on the country roads.

The dog slept at their feet. They talked quietly about the new life they would construct with each other, and when that would happen. Christopher offered to come to Angela's house that night and explain everything to Gregory, but Angela said she couldn't imagine that scenario. 'It would be too much of a shock for him,' she said. Christopher asked her gently how she *wanted* Gregory to find out that she was leaving him for another man, but all she could say in reply was, 'I don't know.'

It began to annoy him. He patiently spelt out the options open to her. 'You could write him a letter, you could telephone, or you could tell him face to face, with, or without me being there. Or, you could just disappear. We can go abroad.'

'Where?' she said. At the moment flight and disappearance seemed the most attractive option open to her.

'You're the travel agent,' he said. 'Where would you like to go?'

'Abroad, somewhere hot. But what would we do with the dog?' She knew she was prevaricating, putting off the evil hour. She answered herself. 'No, we can't go away, we can't leave the dog. I'll tell Gregory tonight. Drop me off at the house and I'll come to you later.'

Christopher sighed with relief and took Angela in his arms. He told her over and over again how much he loved her. The dog whimpered in its sleep. Christopher bent down and stroked it. It woke instantly and licked his hand, then leapt on to his lap. Christopher laughed and cradled the dog in its arms. 'You big baby,' he said and looked at

Angela, wanting her to laugh at the dog, which was grinning and lying on its back with its paws in the air. But she was staring out at the black countryside, rehearsing the words she would use that would break Gregory's heart.

When Gregory heard the throb of the taxi's engine he pulled the sitting-room curtain aside. He dropped it quickly when he saw that the tall man was inside the taxi speaking urgently to his wife. She stood at the open door with her head bowed, listening. Gregory heard the door slam and the taxi drive off. Then he heard Angela's key in the door. He went into the hallway to meet her. When he saw her white distraught face he took pity on her and said, 'I know about the tall man, what's his name?'

'Christopher Moore,' she said. She looked down at the oriental rug. There were intricacies in the patterning that she hadn't noticed before now.

'You used to live with a Christopher Moore,' he said. 'Is it the same one?'

'Yes,' she said. She traced the petals of a flower with the pointed toe of her boot. 'I'm going to live with him again.'

'When?'

'Tonight.'

'I'd better put the kettle on.'

She followed him into the kitchen and watched him filling the kettle under the tap.

'What will I do in this big house?' he said. Then, 'Have you slept with him?'

'Yes.' She wanted to sit down, but thought it best, more polite, to remain standing during the coming interrogation.

'How many times?'

'Three.'

'How long has it been going on?'

'Less than a week.'

'*A week*!'

'Less than.'

'Do you love him?'

'Yes.'

'Do you love me?'

'No.'

She was like a surgeon making an incision without an anaesthetic. It was best to cut quickly and deeply and get it over with.

He hadn't expected her to say 'no'. It had never once crossed his mind that some day Angela wouldn't love him. He was seven years younger than her and more attractive. She was forty-six. She was fat. She was clumsy and vague and she hadn't given him a child. He plugged the kettle in.

'He must be *desperate*,' he said. He wanted to punish her further.

'He *is* desperate,' she said.

She's like a zombie standing there in her coat with her arms hanging down by her sides, he thought. He crossed to the refrigerator and took a bottle of milk from out of the deep shelf inside the door.

'What's he like in bed?' he said.

'I'm going upstairs to get some things together,' she said.

'You're going *nowhere*,' he shouted, and he ran to the kitchen door and slammed it shut and stood in front of it.

'What's he like in bed?'

'Please, Gregory, don't.'

'What's he like in bed?' He was screaming now. She covered her face, hiding from the rawness of his anger. The full milk bottle hit her on the side of her head, and broke on the tiled floor. She lost her footing and fell on to the spreading pool of milk and shards of glass, then he was on top of her, crying and slapping and sobbing that he loved her and begging her not to go. She watched the blood from her forehead insinuate itself into the milk. It looked like a pink river flowing into a white sea. Eventually he grew quiet and lay with his head on her belly. She smoothed his bristly hair and, to comfort him, said, 'He's no good in bed, his penis is too small.'

Gregory lifted his head and said, 'We'd better clean each other up.'

They got up and went upstairs to the bathroom and took their clothes off and examined their bodies under the bright light of the small bulbs set in the ceiling. Like chimpanzees grooming, they removed the almost invisible shards of glass from each other's wounds. Then they climbed into the huge bathtub together and washed away the blood and the milk and the tears and the marriage.

Gregory had been sexually excited during the struggle on the kitchen floor, but the thought of the desolate months ahead of him and the stinging pain from the cuts on his hands, drove all sexual feeling away. As they applied Savlon to their wounds they discussed what to do about their finances. They were both scrupulously fair in the discussion. They moved into their bedroom. Gregory put on his dressing gown and slippers and sat down on the edge of the bed and took a pencil and pad from his bedside drawer. He wrote 'Angela' and 'Gregory' at the top of the page and drew a central line between them. In the half an hour during which she dressed herself and packed the few clothes she was taking with her that night he had divided their property equitably. She agreed to his every suggestion.

She was frantic to leave the house. She didn't trust his apparent calmness and made sure that she kept him in her sight at all times. She didn't dare turn her back on him. When she was ready, she wheeled her small green suitcase out on to the landing and parked it next to her matching overnight bag. Still watching him she went to her jewellery box and tipped the contents into her handbag, then stood in front of him and said, 'Have you retrieved my car keys yet? If you haven't I'll call a cab.' He folded the piece of paper, drew his thumbnail down the crease, then carefully tore the paper in half and gave her the piece headed 'Angela'.

She took it without looking at it, and put it inside her handbag. She used the phone in the bedroom to call a cab and gave a false destination. She didn't want Gregory to overhear and find out where Christopher lived, not yet. She wanted to spend her first full night in Christopher's arms without the fear that Gregory would turn up raging on the doorstep. He carried her suitcase downstairs and left it by the front door.

The door to the understairs cupboard was slightly ajar and she automatically went to close it, but before she did so she saw the stacked-up toys he had bought earlier that day. She saw the doll in its cellophane and cardboard box. As she picked it up its unnaturally blue eyes opened and stared at her. She replaced it on top of the stack and closed the cupboard door.

'Who are the toys for?' she said.

'A kid I know,' he said, and his voice was thick with tears.

Forty-Four

Ken took the remote control out of Tamara's hand and switched off the television. She sat up straight on the sofa knowing that something must be wrong. If somebody wanted to talk they usually pressed the 'mute' button.

'I've got something to tell you, Tammy,' he said. He went to the fish tank and fed the fish, pinching flakes from a little pot and sprinkling them across the surface of the bubbling water. He loved the way the fish swam to the surface. They were dependent on him for their seemingly pointless lives, he thought. He took the top off the bottle of Johnnie Walker and drank heavily, gulping at the amber liquid until his eyes watered. Tamara watched him apprehensively. She hoped he wasn't going to go on about Crackle again, or make her swear on Mum's Bible that she would never see him again.

Ken sat down opposite Tamara and put the bottle on the carpet, between his feet. He took something out of his pocket and showed it to her.

'Do you know what this is?' he said.

She took the thing from him and examined it. It was a plastic cylinder with a padded top. She'd never seen anything like it before.

'No,' she said.

'D'you see that blue sort of circle?'

'Yes.' She wondered if it was a magic trick. He used to make coins come out of his ears when she was a kid.

'Well, Tammy, that blue circle means that you're pregnant.'

She laughed out loud and shook her head. She'd done the same thing when he'd told her that her mother was dead and in the arms of Jesus. He read out loud from the 'Predictor' leaflet, but she said, 'You're making it up, Dad.'

With a superhuman effort he kept his voice even. 'Let's just say that you *are* pregnant Tam, let's just *say*. What would you do about it?'

'What do you mean *do* about it?' she said.

'I mean would you want the baby or would you, you know, get rid of it?'

168

She was amazed that he'd even asked the question. He was the one who'd always said that abortion was murder.

'I couldn't get rid of it. It's wrong.'

Ken shouted, 'I know it's wrong but it has to be done!' He tried again to control his voice, 'Tam, if you get rid of that baby I'll pay for the operation. I'll give you some money and I'll get you a course of driving lessons.'

'No.' She shook her head. 'I couldn't do it, Dad.'

'I'll buy you a car,' he said. 'I'll take you to Raj's garage tomorrow.'

'I'm not pregnant. It must be wind or summat,' she shouted, stroking her stomach. She couldn't be pregnant, not without Crackle's permission.

Ken went into the kitchen and called the emergency doctor service. Perhaps when she'd been told by a professional she would believe that she had a baby inside her.

It was a young red-haired doctor whom neither Ken nor Tamara had seen before. He was very angry at being called out to a non-emergency, but Ken insisted that he examine Tamara. Ken went outside the room whilst Tamara sulkily pulled her clothes down and lay on her back on the sofa.

'She's about six and a half months pregnant. Why isn't she registered with the community midwife?' said the doctor, coming out into the hall, still wearing his green waxed coat.

'She's an ignorant little cow, that's why,' said Ken, angrily.

Six and a half months. It was too late now to intervene in order to save the child from being born.

Tamara passed the two men and went upstairs to the bathroom and locked herself in. Then she pulled her black sweater up and held her belly with both hands and looked into the mirror over the washbasin in triumph. She couldn't wait to tell Crackle the good news.

Later that night, when Ken was asleep, she crept out of the house and went back to the flat. Crackle wasn't there. He'd torn her clothes up and smashed the pots and thrown everything else she'd owned in a pile on the living-room floor: her make-up and tapes and shoes, and the red coat and the hairbrush she'd used when she had long hair. He'd tried to set fire to the pile, the red coat was scorched and the bristles on the brush had melted. She sorted through the mess and found the studded leather wrist band that he'd bought her for a wedding present.

It wasn't damaged and she buckled it on to her wrist. As she was leaving the flat, she noticed an envelope propped up on top of the television. 'Tamara' it said. It was almost the only word she could read.

Tamara hadn't got the key to Ken's door. She had to ring the doorbell and get him out of bed, waking him from a dream in which he was walking arm in arm with Cath in the cemetery where she was buried. He opened the door cautiously, fearing that it was Crackle on the doorstep. Tamara was shivering with cold and excitement, her eyes glittered like black ice. As soon as she was in the narrow hallway, before he could ask where she'd been, she had thrust the letter into his hands and begged him to read it to her. He went upstairs to find his spectacles, taking the letter with him. He switched on the lamp with the pink tasselled shade, which was on Cath's side of the bed, and put his spectacles on. He opened the envelope and took out a sheet of paper torn from a child's exercise book. It was covered in Crackle's backward slanting, spidery scribble.

> Dear Tam, Why won't you talk to me. I have got things to say to you that are important. Bilko has turned against me, I have got to go somewhere else to live, I want you to come with me. I don't know who is reading this to you if it is your dad well he never gave me a chance. Just because I am not like him. Say you will come Tam. We will never get Storme back, so there is just you and me now. Crackle.

Ken folded the letter and put it back into the envelope. He rubbed a hand over his face and got up from the bed. He went downstairs slowly and went into the kitchen where Tamara was standing by the electric kettle on the work top, waiting for it to boil. She had put a tea-bag in each of the two mugs and taken a milk bottle out of the fridge. The glass sugar bowl stood near by. Ken said, 'Right, better read it then.' He took the piece of paper out of the envelope for a second time and what she heard was: 'Dear Tam, Why did it have to end like this? I am sorry but I am going away to live somewhere else. I don't love you any more. I am sorry about hurting Storme, I didn't mean to. Crackle.'

The kettle came to a noisy boil, then switched itself off. Tamara took the letter from Ken's hand and scanned it. She saw her own name Tamara and near the bottom, Storme – but the other scribbled words were incomprehensible to her. She couldn't believe what it said. 'Read it again, Dad,' she said.

Ken had been dreading this, but he managed to approximate much of his previous reading.

'I can't believe he doesn't love me,' she said, turning her stricken face to Ken.

'He admits that he hurt Storme,' said Ken.

'He was heavy-handed that's all,' said Tamara.

'So she didn't fall out of her cot?'

'No,' said Tamara, then she began to cry and repeated, 'I can't believe he don't love me no more.'

Ken tore off a piece of kitchen towel from a pine roller on the wall and gave it to her to wipe her eyes.

'We'd better burn this,' he said. 'If the police found it . . .' She gave the letter back to him and he set fire to it in the stainless-steel sink, using his cigarette lighter. Then he washed the blackened, curling scraps down the plughole using a powerful stream of water from the cold tap.

Forty-Five

Waiting for her was an ordeal. Christopher walked through the rooms of his house, trailed by the dog. He went into the bedroom and checked it. He had remade the bed with clean sheets and a fresh duvet cover, and had positioned the pillows and their clean pillow slips symmetrically against the bedhead. He went into the largest of the spare bedrooms and began to unpack the books from the boxes, taking them to the shelves and squeezing them into any available space. He worked quickly, not allowing himself to look at the titles in case he got seduced into reading. Before long he'd cleared a large space in the middle of the room. When the shelves were crammed full, he took the residue of the books downstairs and started to fill the alcove by the fire where his television and video used to be.

He went into the smaller spare room, where he kept the first editions and more valuable books. He rearranged the shelves to create more space for the books in the booksellers' packages which he'd not yet opened. He looked forward to cataloguing and sorting his collection. He would like Angela to help him.

He found a broom and a dustpan and he swept through the house in honour of Angela. As he did so, he wondered how he could tell Angela about the dead baby he'd found. There was no question, he decided, of him not telling her. One day he intended to tell her everything, however much it frightened or hurt her. He thought that telling the truth was the greatest form of intimacy possible between two people.

When he had finished cleaning he washed himself and combed his hair and sat down in front of the gas fire with the dog. The house was so quiet that it was possible to hear the oven clock ticking from the kitchen. He could hear his elderly neighbour coughing through the party wall, and was glad that he'd escaped such loneliness.

When he heard the taxi turn into the cul-de-sac he went to the front door. He felt a flood of relief when he saw her outline on the back seat. She waved to him. He went down the path to greet her and waited at the kerb with the dog at his side. He cried out, 'Angie!' when he saw the red gash on her forehead, but she wouldn't allow him to look at it in the street.

Between them they carried her luggage inside, then Christopher closed the door to the outside world and held her without speaking until she thought he would never let her go of his own volition. She removed herself gently from him and began to give him a fictitious account of how she had hurt her head and cut her hands. Christopher wouldn't like to hear the truth, she thought.

Gregory had been 'extremely civilised' she said, and showed Christopher the piece of paper where her assets from the marriage were listed in Gregory's looping handwriting. Christopher frowned when he read the last item on the list.

'Have you read this?' he asked, certain by her demeanour that she had not. She took it from him and scanned it quickly until she got to the bottom item which she read again.

No. 24   I intend to commit suicide unless you return to me by 9
         a.m. prompt tomorrow.

They sat down on the bottom step of the stairs and looked at their watches. It was ten minutes to eleven by Christopher's and three minutes past by Angela's. Christopher went through to the kitchen and shouted through that the oven clock said it was *one* minute past eleven. Suddenly the most important thing in the world to them was to find out the exact time. The Speaking Clock told them that the oven clock was correct. They adjusted their watches. 'He won't do it, though,' said Angela.

After his wife had left him Gregory sat under the standard lamp and drank two bottles of Chardonnay, staring at the empty television screen. At midnight he began to clear out the garage. He was furious that so much of her junk had accumulated. He'd never once been able to drive his car into the garage.

He enjoyed the physicality of flinging the stuff into the high-walled garden at the back of the house, regardless of its fragility or of caring where it fell. Occasionally he tortured himself by imagining Angela and Christopher Moore laughing, and naked together, then he would grab the heavy things: old tyres, a sack of sand, an ancient car jack and heave them on to her precious herbaceous borders. It gave him some satisfaction to see the trellis and their climbing plants crack away from the walls. There were many things in there he'd forgotten about: a kite, a paddling pool in a box, a Windsor chair with a broken leg. He found a Swiss Army knife, the Executive, which he thought he'd lost.

The garden security lights went on and off as he came and went. It was after three a.m. before he had cleared enough space to enable him to park his own car inside his own garage.

Christopher and Angela lay on their backs in the dark, talking about Gregory and looking up at the white painted ceiling. The central heating was still on and the bedroom was pleasantly warm. They had kicked the duvet to the foot of the bed and were covered only by a white sheet.

Christopher said, 'You're not going back to him tomorrow, are you?'

'No,' she said. 'I'm going to spend the rest of my life with you.'

She sat up in bed and lit a cigarette. 'He threatened to kill himself once before. I left him for a couple of days after a row. He phoned me and said he'd swallow a lot of paracetamol tablets. I went back to him. I was going to anyway.'

'And had he?' asked Christopher.

'No,' said Angela. 'There weren't even any in the house. I'll phone him at the shop in the morning and ask him about my car keys.' She didn't want to talk about Gregory any more. She asked about Christopher's grandma.

Three years before, Christopher had spent nine hours in a cubicle at the Royal Infirmary watching his grandmother die. She had complained of feeling unwell when he had called in on his way to work that morning. He noticed that she hadn't done her hair, and he suspected that she'd slept in her clothes. Unusually, she had asked him to stay for a while and drink a second cup of tea with her. She'd insisted that he take his coat off. There was a fire smoking in the grate and she had grumbled about the poor quality of the coal she was forced to buy nowadays. They sat either side of the fireplace, in identical wooden armchairs with wine-coloured cushions which he'd once helped her to stuff with grey flock.

'I dreamt about your dad last night,' she said. 'I dreamt that he came home from Canada and I weren't in; I were out, having my hair done.'

Christopher had picked up the poker and poked the fire basket which was clogged with yesterday's ash; another small sign that she was not herself.

'I think about Dad a lot,' said Christopher.

'I think about the other one, just lately,' she'd said, as she watched a few flames struggle to take hold of the lumps of smokeless fuel in the grate.

'What "other one"?' asked Christopher.

'I had another one,' she said.

'No, Grandma,' said Christopher, talking to her as if she were a small child, 'you only had one, *Harry*, my dad, remember?'

She'd shouted at him, 'Don't tell me how many children I had, I had *another* one, before your dad, when I were sixteen.'

Christopher was astonished, both at the anger in her voice, and at what she was telling him. She was known in the family for her prudery and condemnation of sex before marriage. She was still scandalised that Christopher and Angela had once 'lived in sin'.

'What happened to the other one, Grandma?' said Christopher.

She got up from her chair and using the chair arm as a support, shuffled towards the alcove cupboard. He followed her and said, 'Can I help you?'

She ordered, 'Sit down.' He crouched on the edge of his chair and watched her bring the bulging photograph album down from an interior shelf, next to the button tin. A few loose photographs fell out and came to rest on the half-moon-shaped hearth rug, before she was seated again.

She knew the page she wanted, and turned to it immediately. She fumbled with a sheet of cellophane paper and extracted a small brown and white photograph.

'That's me,' she said, 'I were carrying the other one when that were took, I were going on the Sunday school outing.' She passed the familiar photograph to Christopher. He searched it now for signs of pregnancy, but saw only a young ringleted girl wearing a dark dress, a white pinafore and lace-up boots. The day must have been windy because her hair was blowing across her large-featured face, and she was holding on to the brim of a straw hat. She was standing in a brick yard of some kind. She was not smiling. She looked frumpy and awkward.

'We went on a horse and cart to Barrow-on-Soar, and had a picnic next to the river.' She took a tortoiseshell comb out of her stiff black handbag at the side of her chair and began to comb her long hair. 'I didn't enjoy it very much, there were too many midges, they got into your hair, and the wasps were after the jam sandwiches,' she said. She pulled small clumps of grey hair from between the teeth of the comb, rolled them between her fingers and threw the ball on to the fire, where it frizzled into liquid for a second, before disappearing.

'When I got home there was this woman in the house, a Mrs Montague, she was the one who delivered the babies and laid out the bodies. At first I thought that sommat had happened to our dad, or one of my brothers and sisters. The house was *that* quiet. Then my mam told me to go upstairs, put my oldest nightgown on and get into her bed. I still din't know what were coming,' she said to Christopher.

Christopher looked away from the remembered fear in her eyes. He had guessed what was coming and he couldn't bear it. He didn't want to listen. He wanted to put his coat on and leave the house and go to his workshop.

'Mam came in first carrying the bucket. She had some old sheets over her arm, and a bundle of newspapers tucked under the other 'un. I don't know where the newspapers came from . . .'

'It doesn't matter, Grandma,' said Christopher. He wished she'd *do* something with her hair. She looked like a witch with it straggling over her shoulders.

'Mrs Montague come in with a shopping bag over her arm, as if she were on her way to the shops . . . She took a bottle of brandy out of her bag and Mam passed her a glass and she poured it out until the glass were three-quarters full. "Drink it straight down," she said to me. I did as I was told, you did in them days,' she said, almost proudly. 'I'd never tasted alcohol before that day, and it made me gag, and then I felt woozy. They put the old sheets and newspapers under me and my mam put her hand over my mouth and Mrs Montague put something sharp and cold inside my you-know-what. And I screamed and screamed through my mam's hand with the pain. They sat with me right until it got dark, and the baby started to be born. *You'll* never know agony like it,' she said to Christopher accusingly.

'It come out in pieces; they had to fix it together like a jigsaw, to make sure there was nothing left inside me.'

'Oh my God,' said Christopher.

'*God* din't help me,' his grandma said, contemptuously. Her mouth moved, but she wouldn't cry. He wanted to get up and put his arms around her and tell her about *his* baby, the one that Angela had rid herself of, but he forced himself to sit and listen. She tipped her head to one side and began to plait her hair.

'It were never spoken of again, never. The next time I saw Mrs Montague she passed me in the street with just a nod.'

'What about your mam?' said Christopher.

'I've just *said*,' she said irritably. 'It were never spoken of again.'

'Until now,' said Christopher.

'I got septicaemia after,' she said, matter of factly. 'I were in the cottage hospital for six weeks, but I never told them what had happened. When they told me that I couldn't have babies, I was glad.'

'But you *did* have a baby, Grandma; you had Harry, my dad,' Christopher prompted.

She looked at him slyly. '*I* didn't have him,' she said. 'Your granddad was a widower when I met him. Your dad was a year old the first time I saw him. His mam died three weeks after he were born.' She looked hard at Christopher. 'What's up with *your* face?' she said, harshly.

'It's a shock to find out that we're not flesh and blood, Grandma,' he said to her.

'It doesn't matter, does it, lad? We've always been pals, haven't we?' she said.

'Good pals,' said Christopher. He got up and put his coat on and went to his work.

He called in at six o'clock to find her sitting in the same chair. The fire had gone out. She saw him but couldn't speak to him, though her mouth worked constantly. When he held her hands he knew that the strength had gone from them and would never return.

'Stroke,' said the young doctor in Accident and Emergency, 'I'll find her a bed on the ward.'

Christopher waited hours in a cubicle with his grandma, hidden behind blue cotton curtains. As she lay there a violent argument broke out between the casualties of a fight outside a night club. Christopher and she listened as they screamed obscenities and threats from adjacent cubicles. Christopher wept with impotent rage. He had never once used a swear word in front of her. He went outside and begged them to be quiet, but they were drunk and wouldn't listen to him. Probably the last thing she heard before she died was somebody telling Christopher to fuck off.

Forty-Six

Angela woke in the dark and lay awake for a long time. Christopher's sleeping body felt heavy against her. When it became just light enough to see she reached out and took her watch from the bedside table next to her. It was seven-thirty. She re-positioned the watch on the table where she could see it from the bed, and followed the golden second hand around the watch face as it raced towards nine o'clock.

Gregory was having his breakfast at the table that had been the cause of the feud with his sister. He filled a highball glass full of Tia Maria and gulped it down in one, as though it were water. He then wrote his suicide note, using a sheet of Lowood's Linens Limited headed notepaper.

'Angela. There is no point in living without you. Gregory.'

The ultimate punishment, thought Gregory. She'd never live a day without the intolerable weight of guilt on her shoulders. And why should she? She'd as good as murdered him. He wrote another letter to his solicitor:

Dear Mr Jerman,
It is my last wish that my entire estate be left to The Lions Club of Great Britain to do with what they wish. I do not wish Angela Lowood, my adulterous wife to benefit in any way from my death. Should she contest my will I trust you will fight her claim in court with your usual vigour. Thanking you in anticipation,
Yours sincerely,
Gregory Lowood

He then searched for the vacuum cleaner and found it in a cupboard in the utility room. He detached the hose and swore, 'bloody hell' when a cloud of dust and fluff fell out on to his shoes. He took a damp cloth from beside the big porcelain sink where Angela used to soak the houseplants when they went on holiday and wiped his shoes clean. He didn't want to be found looking less than immaculate. He looked at his watch. It was five minutes to nine. His staff would be gathering outside the shop, waiting for him to open up. He didn't trust anybody else with the keys. He went around the house checking that the telephone extensions were working. All were. He wondered where Angela was and what she was doing. Why hadn't she rung and begged him not to take his life? He went out to the garage, taking the vacuum-cleaner hose with him. He averted his eyes from the garden he'd wrecked the night before.

The car was waiting for him. He inserted the snake-like hose through a gap in the back window. He used masking tape and cardboard to fill in any gaps where fresh air might leak inside. He then went back into the house and changed into his wedding suit, which was slightly tight, but he wouldn't be uncomfortable for long, he thought. He pinned the note to the front of his jacket. He went for a last walk around the house. The Lowood name would die with him: his sister had married a man called Porter. He selected a photograph of Angela from the many clustered on the arts and crafts sideboard in the sitting room. She was in evening dress at a Lions Club of Great Britain ladies' night dinner. It had been taken just before she got too fat and became a social embarrassment. She was wearing a red satin evening gown with a pinched-in waist and full skirt. Her breasts swelled above the sweetheart neckline. She was smiling fixedly for the official photographer. Gregory carried the photograph in its silver frame out to the garden. He took one last look at the sky. It was grey. He went into the garage and locked the door. He climbed into the driver's seat and switched the engine on. Radio Four came on automatically; a man was talking about badgers. He turned it off until all he could hear was his own pulse drumming in his ears, and the constant throb of the noise of the engine, amplified in the small space. He arranged the photograph on his lap and prepared himself for death.

Forty-Seven

Angela lay under the sheet, thinking about Gregory until nine-fifteen. Then she leapt out of bed naked and ran down to the hallway, not wanting to stop to put her dressing gown on. She went to the hall table and rang Lowood's Linens. The phone in the shop rang with mournful tones. She waited for a long time before putting the receiver down.

Christopher watched from the top of the stairs. He had just come out of the shower and had a white towel round his waist. He brought her dressing gown down to her and put it round her shoulders.

Angela said, 'He's never, ever late for work.' She took a cigarette out of her dressing gown pocket and lit it with unsteady hands.

'Perhaps the weather's held him up,' Christopher said. 'There's black ice on the roads.'

'No,' she said, dialling the house, 'Gregory makes allowances for things like the weather.'

Christopher listened to the ringing tone with mixed feelings. Angela put the receiver down again.

'He's dead, I know he's dead,' she said.

Christopher put his arms around her and stroked her hair. 'If I thought he was dead, I'd ask you to marry me,' he said. 'But he's not dead, Angela, so I won't.'

He smiled down at her but she wouldn't smile back.

'I must go home,' she said. He stopped smiling and turned away. She ran upstairs and began to fling her clothes on.

He came into the bedroom and grabbed a white shirt from inside the wardrobe.

'You still love him, don't you?'

'No,' she shouted.

'Why didn't you marry *me*?' he asked.

'Oh Chris, not now!'

She was putting on a black tunic and matching wide trousers. She sat down on the bed to fasten her boots.

'I was the wrong class for you, wasn't I?'

'No,' she said. Then, 'Hurry up, Chris.'

He was taking his time in fastening the buttons on his white shirt.

'I remember the night we went out to that restaurant with your friend, Sheila, and her solicitor boyfriend. The waiter asked if we'd like an apéritif and I said, "Yes, I'd like the tomato soup." And the waiter laughed and said, "An apéritif is a drink before the meal, sir." I looked at you and you wouldn't look back. You were ashamed of me, Angie.'

'For Christ's sake, Chris! Not now. Put your shoes on!'

'I suppose Gregory knew what an apéritif was,' he said bitterly, tying his shoelace.

The telephone rang loudly, shocking them both. Angela ran downstairs and snatched it up. It was someone from British Telecom sales. She slammed the phone down, then picked it up again and dialled for a mini-cab.

Christopher came to the top of the stairs wearing a black wool suit with his white shirt. He looks like a funeral director, thought Angela. She paced up and down the hallway.

She phoned the shop twice more and the house three times, but the phone was not picked up. As they hurried away from the house they heard the dog howling.

They could smell the fumes as soon as they got out of the mini-cab and when they were half-way up the drive they could see them, blue and curling through the gap under the garage door.

Angela fumbled with the keys on the keyring, unable to find the right one to unlock the garage. She began to cry and gave the keyring to Christopher. He methodically tried all the Yale keys in the lock. Finally the door sprang open and they were almost overcome by the toxicity of the air inside the garage.

They could see Gregory sitting in his car. His head was resting on the steering wheel. Christopher opened the door, covering his own mouth with his hand, turned off the ignition and went to phone for an ambulance. When it was possible to breathe in the garage without retching Angela opened the passenger door and saw the note pinned to Gregory's jacket. He appeared to be dead. She held him in her arms until Christopher came back.

Between them they dragged Gregory out of the car and into the devastated garden. His face was swollen and the colour of a fresh bruise. Angela bent over him, pinched his nose, opened his mouth and covered it with her own. She blew air into his lungs for as long as she could and when she was unable to carry on Christopher took over.

When the ambulance came there still seemed to be no life inside Gregory's body.

Forty-Eight

Angela hardly left the intensive care unit for a day and a night. She sat at Gregory's bedside and watched him breathe. His face behind the oxygen mask was the colour of blue Stilton.

Each time she moved forward to speak his name or to stroke his bristly hair she was reminded, by the slight pressure against her thigh, of the two cartridge paper notes she had found and stuffed into her trouser pocket. She'd unpinned the one addressed to her from the front of his suit jacket. The other, to his solicitor, she had discovered on the kitchen table propped against a half-empty bottle of Tia Maria.

Since he had been pulled from the car Gregory had not spoken or opened his eyes in response to loud sounds or bright lights. A doctor had jabbed a sterile needle into the soft flesh under his heel but he had not moved his foot.

The hospital chaplain was on his rounds. He approached Gregory's bedside and asked Angela if she would like to join him in a short prayer for her husband's recovery. It would have seemed discourteous to refuse so she closed her eyes and the chaplain said in a voice hardly louder than a whisper: 'Lord, we pray that your servant, Geoffrey will recover and take his place once more in your most blessed world. Amen.'

Angela said, 'Amen'. She was too polite to point out that the Chaplain had called Gregory by the wrong name.

After he had moved on to the next bedside she got up stiffly and went to meet Christopher.

Christopher had called in to see Storme and was astonished and delighted to see that she was sitting up holding a bright pink teddy bear. He hung over the high-sided metal cot and stroked her cheek. He longed to pick her up, but she was still tethered by wires and tubes. Somebody had brushed her hair and gathered it high on her head in an elasticated hair band covered in white satin cord. Her cheeks were flushed pink and he thought that she looked at him with shy recognition. She turned the bear upside down and pulled at a loop on the bear's foot where the washing instructions were printed.

Staff Nurse Fox stood in the doorway waiting to give Storme her medication. Christopher asked, 'What will happen to her, when she's better?'

'She'll go to foster parents,' she said.

'Good,' said Christopher. He kissed his own fingers and touched Storme's head with them and said, 'Goodbye, chick.' He knew that Staff Nurse Fox was impatient for him to leave.

Crackle ran through the quiet Sunday streets of the city centre in a denim shirt and jeans. He'd sold his leather jacket the night before for twenty pounds. The money had bought him a tiny piece of crack which he'd taken in the public toilet outside the bus station. He needed to take more but none of the dealers would give him credit or even let him over the doorstep. He'd rung other crackheads, but nobody wanted to know him. He'd tried to talk to Tamara on the phone, but Ken had put the phone down on him after saying that if he came to the house or tried to contact Tamara the police would be called. He'd been up all night without sleep, having the door slammed in his face. But he knew that Ken drank in the Man at Rest every Sunday dinnertime without fail, and he stopped running and went into a phone box outside the Town Hall and rang Ken's number. Tamara answered at once, and though she'd sworn on her dad's Bible that she would put the phone down immediately without speaking if Crackle rang, she found that she couldn't do it. He sounded desperate. He told her that he was in his shirt-sleeves, he needed a coat, food and drink and crack money. To cheer him up Tamara told him that she was pregnant. She said, 'Dad wanted to pay me to have an abortion, but I said, "No".' There was silence on the other end of the phone, but she knew he was still there, she could hear him breathing.

'Meet me at Veronica's, Tam,' he said. 'This baby's been sent for a purpose.' Crackle left the phone box and stood for a while watching a gang of council workers construct the Christmas tableaux in the square. This year's theme was Peter Pan. As he watched, a cut-out Captain Hook was hauled up to the prow of a plywood pirate ship and fastened into place with strong bolts. He walked out of the square, past the row of cherry trees, whose branches were festooned with small twinkling lights.

He passed the Pizza Hut, where a prosperous looking black family were eating at a table in the window. He took a tortuous detour to avoid passing the Man at Rest and eventually came in sight of the prison and the hospital, and, just beyond them Veronica's, where salvation lay. He could tell it was open; there was a folding sign on the pavement which said, 'Beef/Lamb/Pork/4 Veg/Pie/Ice-cream/£2.39! ! !'

A double-decker bus went by and Tamara shouted, 'Crack!' from an upstairs window. He ran towards the bus stop to meet her. She jumped off the bus before it had come to a stop, and ran along the snow-flaked pavement with her arms outstretched. The wind pressed the long black dress against her thighs and outlined her pregnant belly. The word 'love' came into his mind, but the words he said to her were to do with the more urgent need he had, which was to stop the craving in his body. He was in agony.

'Did you bring some money, Tam?'

'No, I only had the bus fare,' she said. She had searched the house before she left, but Ken had taken every penny out with him; even the little jug on the kitchen shelf in which he saved his twenty-pence pieces was empty.

Crackle let go of her and kicked at a metal litter bin.

'I've brought the book,' she said to his back. She took the child benefit book out of her bag and he snatched it out of her hand and walked away from her, his round shoulders hunched against the cold. She followed him into Veronica's. It was busy for once and they had to wait for a table to be cleared of gravy-stained plates. Eventually, after a young girl smeared a grey cloth over a table for four, they sat down. Crackle couldn't keep his body completely still. His brain was figuring, working out. Who would buy the benefit book? It was worth seventy pounds. If he asked for fifty, would he get it? No, he'd ask for thirty. He would need to start phoning soon. Tamara pretended to read the menu written above the serving hatch. She wanted to talk to him about the letter, and the new baby and Storme, but she was afraid that if she did he would explode. She felt like one of those bomb disposal men she'd seen on the television. One false move and she would be destroyed.

Christopher met Angela at the main entrance to the hospital. She greeted the dog first, then straightened up and took her cigarettes and lighter out of her bag.

'How is he, then?' he said, stroking her shoulder.

'No change.'

'I'm sorry,' he said.

She was having difficulty in lighting her cigarette. He took it from her and put it between his lips, lit it and handed it back to her. They walked across the road to Veronica's. Angela was upset as they passed the window to see that Tamara and Crackle were inside, sitting opposite the only two vacant seats at a table for four. She said, 'Let's go somewhere else, Chris,' but he had already opened the door for her and was waiting for her to go in.

'Do you mind?' said Christopher, nodding towards the empty chairs. Crackle shook his head and Christopher and Angela sat down. Tamara bent down and patted the dog's back. Angela said, to break the tension, 'How's your little girl?'

'She's been took by the Social Services,' she said, looking down at the dog, 'but I'm going to have another baby. I'm six and a half months, I only just found out.'

'Congratulations,' said Angela, automatically. She felt Christopher stiffen beside her. The dog got to its feet and Christopher shouted, 'Sit!' so loudly that other people in the café turned to look at him, their faces bulging with food. The dog turned around three times, then sat down at Christopher's feet.

Christopher said, 'I'll buy that baby you've got inside you.'

He looked at Angela and she looked back at him and nodded.

Crackle said, 'How much?'

'He ain't *serious*, Crack,' said Tamara.

'Yes I am,' said Christopher, quietly.

'So, how much?' said Crackle. He wriggled in his chair.

Angela took her cigarettes out and pulled one out of the packet and lit it and inhaled, hungrily.

Tamara clutched at her belly as though guarding the child inside. Angela's cigarette smoke drifted across to her and she waved it away. Christopher took a wad of £50 notes from the inside pocket of his jacket, and peeled some away, and laid them on the table.

Tamara said, 'I want to keep the baby, Crackle.'

'No you don't, Tam,' said Crackle. 'You're no fucking good at it. You ain't a proper mother. I *know* what a proper mother is.'

Angela thought, *I* won't be any good at it either, I won't be able to love somebody else's baby. She stared at the money on the table, hoping

186

that Crackle would push it back to Christopher, but he picked it up and counted it.

'Two hundred and fifty quid,' he scoffed. 'That ain't enough.'

'You'll get that every week until the baby's born, and on that day, you'll get three thousand pounds, and we'll never see either of you again.'

Tamara looked at Angela hard-faced and said, 'I am a proper mother, and when this baby's grown up, it'll *know* and it'll come looking for me, just like Storme will.'

Forty-Nine

Christopher waited until Angela was in the bath before going out into the garden. He listened to the sounds of her washing herself, then pushed the terracotta pot aside. He took a chisel from the shed and levered up the flagstone. Using all his strength he lifted it, then dragged it and leaned it against the fence. He recovered the shoe box from the earth, dragged the flagstone back and dropped it into its place.

He took the shoe box into the shed and put it into the old brown shopping bag that his grandma had used daily for thirty years. He hadn't been able to throw it away. There were indentations of her fingers on the leather handles. He hung the bag on the back of the shed door, closed it, then put the terracotta pot back in place.

He looked up at the bedroom: the curtains were shut. Angela was drying her hair. He could hear the whine of the hairdrier she'd brought with her and laid out on top of the chest of drawers, together with her jars and bottles and brushes and cosmetics. It had delighted him to see her mark her territory in his bedroom.

When Angela had dried her black hair and dressed herself, she went into the living room and stroked the spines of his books. When they had lived together seventeen years ago she had been surprised by the number of books he had brought home. Hardly a day went by when he didn't produce a book from the pocket of the voluminous donkey jacket he wore to work. He spent most of his short lunch breaks in second-hand bookshops. She'd once laughed at him and called him, Jude the Electrician.

She looked along the top row: Beckett, Barnes and Bennett, stood next to Haggard, Heroditus and Hardy. She began to rearrange the books and put them into strict alphabetical order. When he came in and saw her he was moved almost to tears.

There was a funeral about to take place at the Waterloo Road Cemetery. Christopher and Angela sat in her car and watched as a beetle-black hearse with a wreath-covered coffin inside drew up outside the arched door of the chapel. Behind, looming over the tiled roof, was the tall red-brick crematorium chimney from which grey smoke drifted. A muddle of gravestones surrounded them on all sides. In the distance a small mechanical earth digger dipped in and out of a rectangular hole, making a grave by removing dark brown earth and piling it into a heap at the side.

They had brought flowers with them: stargazer lilies. Their perfume was intoxicating in the confinement of the Volvo. A procession of cars drove slowly up the inclination of the drive. Angela felt Catherine's warmth beside her but she couldn't see or hear her.

'Catherine's here, Chris,' she said. 'Can you feel her?'

'No,' he said. 'But I wish I could.'

Christopher watched as the man operating the digger climbed out of the cab and walked off among the gravestones in the far distance. He said to Angela, 'Stay inside the car, Angie.'

He picked up his grandma's bag from the back seat and got out of the car. He walked over the brow of a gentle hill and wandered amongst the ancient gravestones, looking for a resting place in consecrated ground for the little one he'd found in the ditch. He found a large enough niche under a crumbling statue of an angel holding a prayer book. He gathered bits of old masonry and piled them around the gaps until the bag and its contents were hidden.

He didn't know what to say, apart from 'Rest in peace, chick.' He stood for a few moments, memorising the location, though he doubted if he would ever return. A new life was beginning for him. There was only Catherine to say goodbye to now.

As he drew nearer to the car he could see that Angela was watching him anxiously. He hadn't told her about the baby in the ditch. He wouldn't now. It was a secret he would take with him to his own grave.

They waited until the mourners and the coffin had gone inside the chapel and the door had been closed. Then Christopher led Angela around the back of the building to a door which said 'No Admittance'. They stood on either side of the door. They heard a man's echoing voice, then music and tentative singing. 'Are you cold, Angie?' said Christopher to her. He could see that she was trembling. He pulled her towards him, the orange pollen from the lilies he was carrying stained the front of her navy coat.

'Have you thought of what to say?' she asked him.

'Nothing good enough,' he said. 'Have you?'

'No,' she said.

When they heard the car doors slamming at the front of the building and saw the mourners drive off, Christopher knocked on the door. It was opened by a young man with his hair in a pony tail. He was wearing a brown overall over his sweatshirt and jeans. He looked astonished to see them there.

'You want the other door,' he said.

'No,' said Christopher, pushing past him and pulling Angela with him, 'this is the right place. Please, just give us one minute.'

It was hot inside the white painted room. At the far end, set into the wall was a glassed-in roaring bonfire; the incinerator.

Christopher and Angela walked up to it and laid the flowers at its base. Christopher said, 'You're our Catherine, and we'll never forget you.' Angela closed her eyes and tried hard to summon up a picture of Catherine's lovely face. She had it for a moment, but then it started to elude her and by the time they were leaving the incinerator room together it had gone.

February

There was an east wind blowing on the night Tamara went into labour in the rambling Victorian house where Christopher and Angela now lived. The doors and windows shook as the baby fought to take its place in the world. The wind howled around the corners of the house and through the branches of the trees in the garden.

Christopher and Angela wandered through the half-decorated, uncurtained rooms. The dog followed them. The wind hurled leaves, twigs and snowflakes at the windows. After three hours they climbed the stairs, leaving the dog asleep in the kitchen. They went into the bedroom, where Tamara lay on the bed in a tangle of sheets crying for her mother. Christopher asked the midwife, 'How much longer?'

'A while yet,' she said.

They went into the room they had prepared for the baby and checked once more that everything was in its place. They heard a loud crack as a branch split from a tree. Christopher pulled up the nursery blind with its Winnie the Pooh design and they looked out. The wind was making patterns of swirling snow.

Crackle sat downstairs at the table in the large kitchen, smoking and fiddling with the rings on his fingers. Gregory had been drawn up next to him in a customised chair with a built-in tray. He was assembling a jigsaw meant for six-year-olds. Occasionally he would whimper and hold out a piece to Crackle and Crackle would slot it in place impatiently, saying quietly, 'Fucking baby.'

The baby boy cried the moment he left Tamara's body. He was still attached to the milky green cord when Christopher crouched down at the side of the bed and cupped him in his hands. Angela looked at the tiny infant. It was like looking at a miniature Crackle; there was the same frowning brow. Tamara strained up to see her son, then dropped back in exhaustion. When she next woke up she heard the baby crying in a distant room.

Next morning, after the midwife had gone, Crackle counted and recounted the money Christopher had placed on the kitchen table and stuffed the bundle of notes into the pocket of his jeans. He put on his new leather jacket and zipped it up. He watched Angela hold a drinking cup with a spout to Gregory's lips.

'Here's your tea, Greg,' she said.

'Right, I'm off,' Crackle said. 'I'll be back for Tamara next week.'

Christopher couldn't put the baby down. He cradled him in his arms, wrapped in a white shawl. He went to the top of the stairs and listened. He hoped that Crackle had taken his money and gone. Crackle opened the kitchen door. The dog woke up and followed him out into the hallway. When it saw Christopher with the baby it began to growl at the back of its throat. Barking and snarling, it crept up the stairs. When it reached the top it leapt into the air and snarled at the baby. Angela screamed.

Christopher held the baby tight to his chest. He covered its head with his hands, and kicked the squealing dog down the stairs. 'Keep it away from the baby,' he shouted.

Crackle took the dog's lead from a hook on the wall and clipped it on to the dog's collar.

'I'll take it off your hands,' he said.

Neither Christopher nor Angela spoke. Crackle opened the front door and walked out into the snow-filled whirlwind.

Christopher handed the baby to Angela. He ran out on to the path and stared after them. Within moments the dog and its new master had disappeared behind a thick, soft curtain of driving snow.